PRAISE

...ਾਂ S ਾਂ

ONTH PICK

K AWARD NOMINEE

R MEDAL NOMINEE

"A gripping middle school adventure." —*The Advocate*

★ "Levine has created a masterwork of mystery that slowly unravels as Claudia learns more about her father's life . . . The biggest trick is Levine's ability to keep the characters both likable and realistic . . . Both an excellent read and an excellent puzzle." —*Kirkus Reviews*, starred review

"Readers are treated to a fast-paced narrative filled with feeling and subtle family tensions. Levine's clever mixture of modes—including screenplay, transcripts, text threads, emails, receipts, and first-person narration from Claudia—illustrate beautifully the ways multiple perspectives on a subject can provide a nuanced, vibrant picture." —*School Library Journal*

"*The Jigsaw Jungle* is a triumph of a book, portraying sensitive family dynamics in a loving, engaging way." —*BookPage*

"Through the story's patchwork format, Levine reveals characters' inner complexities while maintaining tension and uncertainty leading up to the story's moving revelation. This taut mystery is also a portrait of a family coming to terms with truth and identity." —*Publishers Weekly*

"Ingeniously plotted middle-grade novel by Kristin Levine . . . Develops tween and adult characters with compassion and depth, as they evolve a better understanding of a family that can be 'both great and broken, all at the same time.'" —*The Washington Post*

Also by Kristin Levine

the JIGSAW JUNGLE

Kristin Levine

putnam

G. P. PUTNAM'S SONS

G. P. PUTNAM'S SONS
An imprint of Penguin Random House LLC, New York

First published in the United States of America by G. P. Putnam's Sons,
an imprint of Penguin Random House LLC, 2018
First paperback edition published 2021

Visit us online at penguinrandomhouse.com

THE LIBRARY OF CONGRESS HAS CATALOGED THE HARDCOVER EDITION AS FOLLOWS:
Names: Levine, Kristin (Kristin Sims), 1974– author.
Title: The jigsaw jungle / Kristin Levine.
Description: New York, NY : G. P. Putnam's Sons, [2018]
Summary: Claudia Dalton, twelve, embarks on an unexpected treasure hunt that she hopes will bring
her missing father home and heal whatever is wrong with her family. Told through notes, emails, audio
and video transcripts, and more from Claudia's scrapbook.
Identifiers: LCCN 2018008297 | ISBN 9780399174520 (hardback) |
ISBN 9780698193987 (ebook)
Subjects: | CYAC: Mystery and detective stories. | Missing persons—Fiction. | Secrets—Fiction. |
Jigsaw puzzles—Fiction. | Family problems—Fiction. | Scrapbooks—Fiction. | BISAC: JUVENILE
FICTION / Mysteries & Detective Stories. | JUVENILE FICTION / Family / Marriage & Divorce. |
JUVENILE FICTION / Lifestyles / City & Town Life.
Classification: LCC PZ7.L57842 Jig 2018 | DDC [Fic]—dc23
LC record available at https://lccn.loc.gov/2018008297
Printed in the United States of America

ISBN 9780147516237

10 9 8 7 6 5 4 3 2 1

Design by Eileen Savage
Text set in Arno Pro

For Charlotte and Kara

PART 1

The Piece

I USED TO THINK that life was like a puzzle, and if I was organized and worked really hard, I could make all the pieces fit neatly together.

Turns out, I was wrong.

This scrapbook tells the story of how I learned that. It's full of emails and phone conversations, receipts and flyers. Transcripts of old home movies that I typed up. It's the story of how we lost my dad and how we found him again, all organized in a binder with headings and labels, colored tabs and archival scrapbooking tape.

Because, if you ask me, there's nothing like a good list to make you feel calm and in control. Guess I'm just weird that way. I needed to put this all in one place, to see how the clues and pieces all came together to reveal the truth about me and my family.

And if there's only one thing you learn about me from this collection of documents (and I hope there's not just one, but if there is just one), it's this:

I really do love a good puzzle.

Claudia Dalton

⊠

From: Jeffery Dalton <jeffdalton327@gmail.com>
Date: Friday, June 26, 2015 4:55 PM EST
To: Claudia Dalton <claudiadalton195@gmail.com>, Jennifer Dalton <jennydalton431@gmail.com>
Subject: Will be home late

My favorite girls,

Something came up while I was at work. Not quite sure when I'll be home. Don't wait up!

Love you both,

Dad

Claudia Dalton's Cell Phone | Friday, June 26, 2015, 5:03 p.m.

PHONE TRANSCRIPT

Mom: Hello?

Claudia: Dad said he had to work late. When are you going to be home?

Mom: Um, might be 7:30.

Claudia: But Dad was going to drive Kate and me to the movies! It starts at 7:30.

Mom: Do you mind missing the previews?

Claudia: Yes. And I can't sit in the front row because you know I get a crick in my neck.

Mom: Well, I'm sorry, Claudia, but my big conference is in ten days . . . Why can't Dad take you? I thought this was his last teacher workday before summer vacation.

Claudia: I don't know. He just emailed that something came up.

Mom: Huh. Maybe Kate's mom can take you.

Claudia: She has a project she's trying to finish before she goes on maternity leave.

Mom: That's right! When's the baby due?

Claudia: Couple of weeks.

Mom: Give her my best.

Claudia: Okay. But what about the movies?

Mom: I can pick you up afterward, but—

Claudia: It's fine, Mom. We'll walk.

Mom: Sorry, sweetie. Text me when you're done.

Claudia: Will do.

Mom: Love you!

Claudia: Love you too. Bye.

Claudia Dalton's Cell Phone | Friday, June 26, 2015, 5:11 p.m.

KATE

Hey, BFF?

Sup

Itsy-bitsy change in plans

What?

How do you feel about walking?

Claudia!

Sorry
My dad flaked
Mom working late

Ugh. Mine too

Could your dad . . .

Haha
You know he's never home before 8

So we walk?

Yup

Meet at your place? 6:30?

See you then

WHEN I WOKE up the next morning something felt wrong, but I didn't know what it was. I walked into the kitchen and put some bread into the toaster. I got the paper from the front porch and glanced at the headlines: "Gays' right to wed affirmed," "For Obama, a day of triumph, grief and grace," "Dozens killed in terror attacks on 3 continents." (Why did we still get the paper anyway? Couldn't my parents read it online like everybody else?!) I smeared peanut butter and jelly on my toast.

And then I saw it. My father's favorite mug. The one he used for tea every morning. Sitting on the counter, clean and untouched.

From: Claudia Dalton <claudiadalton195@gmail.com>
Date: Saturday, June 27, 2015 10:30 AM EST
To: Jeffery Dalton <jeffdalton327@gmail.com>
Subject: Where are you?!

Dad,

Why didn't you come home last night?!!!

I'm really freaking out. Did you drop your phone in the toilet again? Did you have a car accident? Did you run away to join the circus?!

Mom says she's sure there's some really lame, normal explanation. Like maybe you went bowling with the young teachers from school and had too many beers and decided to crash on someone's couch and you thought you'd texted us, but there was no signal in the bowling alley and you didn't notice the message had failed to send. Even though I've shown you about 500 times how to check it.

But I think she's lying because Mom spent all morning scrubbing the kitchen floor. You know Mom. Unless we're having a party, she only cleans when she's angry or nervous.

Anyway, call us!!!

Love, Claudia

Claudia Dalton's Cell Phone | Saturday, June 27, 2015, 2:14 p.m.

Mom: Hello—

Claudia: Mom, has he called?

Mom: No. Are you still at the pool with Kate?

Claudia: Yeah. They invited me to stay for dinner too.

Mom: Okay. That's fine.

Claudia: Have you called the police yet?

Mom: Yes, Claudia. They said we have to wait twenty-four hours before filling out a missing persons report.

Claudia: Oh.

Mom: Wait, I'm getting another call!

Claudia: Is it Dad?

Mom: No. No, it's your grandfather. I called him earlier.

Claudia: That means you think it *is* serious!

Mom: I'm just covering all the bases.

Claudia: But, Mom . . .

Mom: I'll let you know if I hear anything. I gotta go.

PHONE TRANSCRIPT

Jenny Dalton's Cell Phone | Saturday, June 27, 2015, 2:16 p.m.

Mom: Have you heard anything, Walter?

Papa: No, I was just checking in with you.

Mom: Oh.

Papa: This is so strange. Was Jeff having any problems?

Mom: No.

Papa: You don't sound certain.

Mom: Well, he was acting a little distant lately. But I thought that was because of Lily. I thought it was normal.

Papa: Grief is normal. Disappearing is not.

Mom: I know. I need to call some more friends and ...

Papa: Let me know if you hear anything.

Mom: I will.

Sp-67 (Rev. 1-1-2006)

Virginia Missing Persons Information Clearinghouse Report

INVESTIGATING OFFICER Maria Campbell	DATE REPORTED: June 28, 2015 8:14 AM DATE ENTERED VCIN/NCIC: VIC NO:

PART 1

*Agency Submitting Report:				*ORI No:

*Last Name Dalton	*First Name Jeffery	Middle Name Robert	Suffix	*Sex M	*Race White

Place of Birth: Bakersfield, CA   *Date of Birth: 6/20/1974

*Height 6 ft. 2 in.	*Weight 205 Lbs.	*Eye Color ☐ Black ☐ Maroon ☐ Green ☐ Gray ☐ Hazel ☐ Multicolor ☐ Pink	☐ Blue ☒ Brown ☐ Unknown	* Hair Color ☐ Black ☐ Blond ☐ White ☐ Sandy ☒ Brown ☐ Gray ☐ Red ☐ Pink

Complexion	☒ Fair/Light ☐ Black ☐ Medium ☐ Albino ☐ Dark ☐ Olive ☐ Ruddy ☐ Sallow ☐ Yellow ☐ Lt. Brown ☐ Med. brown ☐ Dark Brown	Scars, Marks, Tattoos and Other Characteristics Scar on left leg under knee; no tattoos

Fingerprint Classification:	Social Security Number: xxx-xx-xxxx

Operator's License Number B2987	O.L. State VA	Date of Expiration 6/12/19	DNA ☐ Yes ☒ No Location of DNA:

*Date of Last Contact: 6/26/15	*Originating Agency Case Number:

Fingerprints Available ☒ Yes ☐ No Location of the Fingerprints Richmond Public Schools	Photo Available ☒ Yes ☐ No Photo Received ☒ Yes ☐ No Photo sent to the State Police ☒ Yes ☐ No	Dental Records ☒ Yes ☐ No Location of the Dental Records Smile Time Dentistry

Blood Type: O+	Body X-Rays Available ☐ Full ☐ Partial ☒ No	Location of the X-Rays:

Medication Required ☐ Yes ☒ No	Medication Type	Medical Condition ☐ Yes ☒ No If Yes, what type:

Person Who Is Reporting Subject Missing:

Last Name Dalton	First Name Jennifer	Middle Name Ann

Relationship to Missing Person: wife

Address: 3457 Fast Run Trail Richmond, VA   Contact Telephone: 804-555-3948

Telephone # of Investigating Agency (accessible 24 hours) Area Code ( )	Authority for Release ☐ Yes ☐ No

Last Seen in Company of: NAME(S)		Sex	Race
(1)			
(2)			

MISCELLANEOUS DATA
(information which may assist in identification: nickname, associates, direction of travel, hairstyle, clothing, etc.)

| |
| |

VEHICLE INFORMATION

License Plate Number	State	Year of Exp.	Lic. Type	VIN
Vehicle Year 2010	Make Toyota	Model Prius	Style	Color Blue

Corrective Vision Prescription: Wears glasses
Jewelry Type and Description:

PART III

I certify the person described in Part I is missing and that the information I have furnished is true and correct to the best of my knowledge and belief.

Janfer Dalt	6/28/15	wife
Signature	Date	Relationship

PART IV

I authorize any law enforcement official to use photographs and/or any other identifying information I have provided in any manner they deem necessary in attempting to locate the person I am reporting missing.

Janfer Dalt	6/28/15	wife
Signature	Date	Relationship

Virginia Missing Person Information Clearinghouse
Virginia State Police
Criminal Justice Information Services Division
P. O. Box 27472
Richmond, Virginia 23261-7472

*** IMPORTANT ***

PLEASE ATTACH A CURRENT PHOTOGRAPH OF THE MISSING PERSON TO THIS FORM

EARLY SUNDAY MORNING, so early it was still dark, I woke up and couldn't fall back asleep. When I went into the kitchen for some breakfast, I found Mom already there.

She was sitting at the kitchen table, picking slips of paper out of a Mason jar. I knew what they were: messages my father had left in my lunch.

Have a great first day of school!

Good luck on your science test.

Break a leg in your history skit!

Dad had put notes in my lunch for years, not every day, but a couple times a week. I always brought them home and stuffed them into the jar as I cleaned out my lunch box.

At least I had until a few months ago. Billy Peterson had caught me reading one, snatched it out of my hand, and spent the rest of the day repeating, "I love you, sweetie! Have an amazing day!" in a fake, high-pitched voice. I'd marched home and told Dad I was too old for notes in my lunch anymore.

I felt awful about that now. Had I hurt Dad's feelings? Was he mad at me? Mom and I pulled note after note out of the Mason jar until they covered the kitchen table.

When we were done, Mom finally admitted that she was worried too. She cooked breakfast, eggs that neither of us ate, and we filled out the missing persons report together. I looked through my phone and found three current photos of Dad to give to the police. I also found the following video, in case they wanted to put it on TV or anything.

INT. KITCHEN—NIGHT

The room is full of people. Streamers hang from the ceiling and a bunch of balloons are tied to one chair. Claudia's father, Jeff, stands next to the balloon chair. His hair is dark and he wears brown glasses. He has on a blue dress shirt, khaki pants, and a novelty math tie that says $C = 2\pi r$. Jeff is chatting with Kate and her mom, Mrs. Anderson. Kate wears a silly hat with candles, which she takes off and puts on Jeff's head. Her mother wears a dark blue maternity dress that clings to her belly.

JENNY (Off-Screen)

Time for cake!

The lights suddenly go out.

Claudia's mother carries a beautifully decorated round cake with two number candles, 4 and 1, on the top. She looks as if she's come straight from work. She has dark blond, shoulder-length hair, and is wearing a silk blouse and a pencil skirt. Everyone starts to sing.

Jeff smiles patiently until they're done. Then he closes his eyes for a moment, making a wish. He opens his eyes and blows out the candles. Everyone cheers.

Jenny leans over and gives him a kiss.

JENNY (CONT'D)

Happy birthday, sweetie.

I T WAS STRANGE to see my father on the video. I couldn't help thinking that if I walked out of the kitchen and into the living room, my father would be there, reading the paper.

There were no other videos of my father on my phone, just a few clips of Kate and me and a couple of other girls from school at a sleepover, lip-synching to songs and trying out crazy hairdos.

I told Mom we needed to get out our home movies—the clip was kind of dark and a little blurry for television—but she said Dad had taken most of our videos to his parents' house when Nana was sick. She'd felt too bad from the chemo to do much except lie on the couch, and watching videos of me always cheered her up.

Mom promised to see what else she could find. But I still felt disappointed. I wanted to see those videos now. I wanted more notes in my lunch. I wanted to see my father again, even if it was only for a moment on a screen.

Claudia Dalton's Cell Phone | Monday, June 29, 2015, 10:49 a.m.

Kate: Did you hear from your dad yet?

Claudia: No.

Kate: That's so strange. Everything seemed normal at his birthday party last week!

Claudia: I know. Do you think he had an accident?

Kate: Didn't the police check the hospitals?

Claudia: Yeah. No John Does matching his description.

Kate: Well, that's good.

Claudia: Do you think he was, like, a secret drug user or something?

Kate: Your dad?!

Claudia: Yeah, you're right. He doesn't even drink coffee.

Kate: Maybe he was kidnapped.

Claudia: Who would kidnap a guy who is 6'2"?

Kate: It could happen.

Claudia: I guess.

Kate: It's just so odd. Your dad is, like, Mr. Dependable. Do you remember last year when I forgot my permission slip?

Claudia: Yeah.

Kate: My mom was in a meeting. My dad said it was "too bad" I wasn't more responsible. Your dad said, "Sure, I'll swing by your house on my lunch hour and pick it up."

Claudia: I remember.

Kate: That meant so much to me! I mean, if my dad disappeared, I wouldn't be so surprised. He's always at work anyway. But your dad . . .

Claudia: You're making me feel worse, Kate!

Kate: Sorry. Want to come to the pool? Might help get your mind off things.

Claudia: Thanks, but no. I'm gonna stay home with Mom. In case we hear anything.

Kate: Okay. Text me later.

Claudia: Will do.

Walter Dalton's Cell Phone | Monday, June 29, 2015, 1:35 p.m.

[RECORDING BEGINS]

I wish you were here, Lily. Our son has been missing for three days now. It's been awful. A couple of your friends from book club called to check on me. But I didn't return their messages.

I did finally go see that geriatric grief specialist you found for me before you died. The guy wasn't too much of an idiot, I guess. Though he did tell me to start a diary of my thoughts and feelings. What a bunch of touchy-feely crap! I told him I stopped writing reports when I retired. But he insisted, and I agreed to try talking to my phone. Hence, the voice memos.

Nah, I can't do this. This is the stupidest idea I've ever—

[RECORDING ENDS]

MOM FOUND A box of old keepsakes way back in her closet. There was a program from the musical *Camelot*—Dad had taken her on one of their first dates. Under the program was a pile of postcards, bound together with a rubber band. Mom blushed when I picked them up. "Dad sent me one every single week of junior year when I was spending a semester in France." Each postcard had a quote on it:

"How do I love thee? Let me count the ways."
Elizabeth Barrett Browning

"Shall I compare thee to a summer's day?"
William Shakespeare

"O my Luve is like a red, red rose."
Robert Burns

In the box were also two videotapes. We watched them together that afternoon, curled up on the couch. The first was their wedding video. Mom said her favorite part was when the minister messed up the vows. "It broke the tension. Then Dad and I could just relax and enjoy the ceremony." The second was of my fourth birthday. It should have been with the tapes Dad had taken to Nana, but I guess it had been placed in the wrong box.

INT. CHURCH—DAY

A younger Jenny wears a white dress and veil. She's smiling and clutching a bouquet of flowers. A younger Jeff stands beside her in a dark suit. He's pale and serious. His hands are trembling. A female minister stands between them, officiating.

> MINISTER
>
> Thank you for that lovely reading. Now it's time for the vows.

A hush falls over the crowd.

> MINISTER (CONT'D)
>
> Do you, Jeffery Robert Dalton, take Jennifer Ann Thompson to be your lawfully wedded husband?

Everyone laughs, including Jenny and Jeff. Jeff's hands finally stop shaking.

> MINISTER (CONT'D)
> (smiling)
> I'm sorry! I mean your wife.

> JEFF
>
> I do.

Jenny takes Jeff's hand and squeezes it. He smiles.

———

INT. KITCHEN—DAY

Claudia wears a frilly dress and a party hat. There's a half-eaten cake on the table with the words *Happy 4th Birthday, Claudia* written in pink icing. She's right in the middle of opening presents.

                    DAD

        Now, this is a special one. It's something my mother
        taught me to do.

Claudia looks at Nana, who is standing nearby.

                    CLAUDIA

        Nana.

                    DAD

        Yes, Nana is my mother. And now I want to teach
        you.

                    CLAUDIA

        What?

                    DAD

        Open it.

Claudia rips off the paper.

                    CLAUDIA
                   (confused)

        It's a puzzle.

                    DAD

        A big-girl puzzle. With one hundred pieces.

                    CLAUDIA

        Really?! A hundred?

                    NANA

        Oh, Jeff, I think that's too many for her.

                    CLAUDIA
          No! I'm a big girl.

Everyone laughs.

                    ————

INT. KITCHEN—LATER
The table is cleared of cake and dishes. Jeff and Claudia sit close
together. Claudia listens intently to everything her father says.

                    DAD
          First, you dump all the pieces onto the table. Then you
          turn them picture side up and sort them into edge
          and middle pieces.

                    CLAUDIA
          Edge?

                    DAD
          The edge pieces have a side that is straight.

He picks one up and hands it to her. She runs her little finger
across it.

                    CLAUDIA
          I feel it!

                    ————

INT. KITCHEN—LATER
Claudia leads her mother into the kitchen.

                    CLAUDIA
          Keep your eyes closed!

                         MOM

     My eyes are closed.

She stops at the table.

                        CLAUDIA

     Now open.

Her mom does. The puzzle, "Animal Alphabet," is completed on
the table.

                    CLAUDIA (CONT'D)

     Ta-da!

                         MOM

     Did you do this?!

                        CLAUDIA

     All by myself. Dad only helped a little.

                         MOM

     Wow!

Jeff ruffles her hair and smiles.

MY PARENTS LOOKED so young at their wedding, it was almost like they were different people. And I barely remembered getting that first puzzle. Puzzles were something my father and I had done together, almost every weekend, for years. Until, well, until last year, I guess, when I started middle school and I wanted to hang out with my friends more.

Watching that video and seeing how happy we had been, I worried that my dad's disappearance had something to do with me. I thought about saying something to Mom then, but the phone rang. It was the police. They'd found some surveillance footage from the bank and an email.

While Mom was talking to the police, I went to get the mail.

EXT. BANK OF AMERICA—NIGHT

The date/time stamp in the lower right-hand corner reads: 2015/06/26 17:25:03. A tall man in khaki pants and a light blue dress shirt approaches the ATM. He swipes his card and enters his PIN. He withdraws the maximum daily allowance of $800 from his checking account. He does not request a receipt.

No one is visible in the frame with him.

The next person to use the ATM is an old woman with a cane, approximately three minutes later.

From: Uber Receipts <do-not-reply@uber.com>
Date: Friday, June 26, 2015 6:07 PM EST
To: Jeffery Dalton <jeffdalton327@gmail.com>
Subject: Your Friday evening trip with Uber

$11.45

Fare Breakdown
Base Fare: 2.00
Distance: 5.06
Time: 3.39
Subtotal: $10.45
Safe rides fee: 1.00

Charged:
Personal XXXX-XXXX-XXXX-XX45 $11.45

● 5:45 PM | 20 Division Blvd.

● 6:05 PM | Greyhound Bus Station

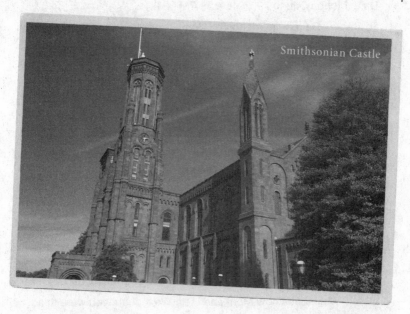

I need a little time to
think some things over.
Spending a few days
in New York and then
going to visit an old
friend. I'm sorry. Will
be in touch again soon.

          Love, Dad

Jenny and Claudia Dalton
3457 Fast Run Trail
Richmond, VA

No.13

EMAIL

From: Claudia Dalton <claudiadalton195@gmail.com>
Date: Monday, June 29, 2015 2:33 PM EST
To: Jeffery Dalton <jeffdalton327@gmail.com>
Subject: At least you're not dead

Dear Dad,

    You're a jerk! A big fat jerk!! How could you disappear on Mom and me like that?! I'm glad you're not dead, but I'm so ANGRY at you!! What do you need to think over? Are you in the mafia? Did you rob a bank? Did you kill someone? Why won't you just tell us what's wrong??

    Do you remember when I was seven and we were at the movies and you fell asleep? I got hungry, so I took some money from your wallet and went to go get popcorn. When you woke up, you didn't know where I was and you were so terrified, you nearly had a heart attack. Well, that's how Mom and I felt. We thought you were dead!

    Just come home and I'm sure we can figure this all out. It can't be that bad! Isn't that what you always say to me?!

Love, Claudia

Mom: Did you get the picture of the postcard I attached to the email?

Papa: Yes. What did the police say?

Mom: They said it supports their theory that he left voluntarily. He left his car at school, paid cash for his bus ticket. None of the other teachers noticed anything wrong. According to the police, there's nothing more they can do.

Papa: What?

Mom: Apparently, it's not illegal to walk out on your wife and daughter.

Papa: What?!

Mom: I'm just telling you what they said.

Papa: So what do we do now?

Mom: Do you have any idea where he might be? Any old friends in New York?

Papa: Jeff doesn't have a lot of friends.

Mom: I know. Did anything seem off the last time you saw him?

Papa: I haven't seen him since Lily's funeral. That was four months ago.

Mom: He stayed a week afterward. What did you all do?

Papa: Nothing! Boxed up her clothes. Threw some stuff out. Jeff spent a lot of time in the attic, organizing his old puzzles. He stayed up late watching TV.

Mom: There's got to be something.

Papa: There's a box of stuff in his old closet. Yearbook, old papers, nothing that would help.

Mom: It'll be okay, Walter. We just need to be patient and—

Papa: Patient?!

Mom: What else can we do?

Papa: [SILENCE]

Mom: We'll find him, Walter.

Papa: I hope so.

Walter Dalton's Cell Phone | Tuesday, June 30, 2015, 8:45 a.m.

VOICE MEMO

[RECORDING BEGINS]

A postcard?! One lousy postcard. That's all he's sent.

I can't believe this. I wish you were here, Lily. We need your optimism. And yet, part of me is glad you're not around to experience this. It's like when you got sick and there was nothing I could do. I hate feeling so helpless.

The doctor said I should shake up my routine, try something different. I guess I'll look through the box in the closet. I have to do something! Maybe Jenny can be patient, but I . . .

[RECORDING ENDS]

GEORGE WASHINGTON
JUNIOR HIGH SCHOOL

1987

Inside the front cover are a bunch of handwritten messages.

To Jeff,

It's been nice knowing you this year.
Have a great summer. Let's play mini
golf again soon.

Steve

To Jeff,

You are my best friend. Would have
been an awful year if I hadn't met
you! Have a terrific summer and come
visit me next year!

Brian

To Jeff,

I haven't gotten to know U that well this year.
I hope I get to know U better next year.

Amanda

To Jeff,

Better than elementary school, huh?! Thanks
for the food and answers. And remember—
always write your name in your underwear!!

Paul

MARCHING BAND

Jeffery Dalton, clarinet

7TH GRADE HISTORIANS

This year the 7th graders each put together a time capsule—maybe they put in the front page of the newspaper, or even a pair of orange Reeboks. Just don't forget where you bury it—you might want to dig it up in 30 years!

From: InterContinental Geneve <do-not-reply@geneve.com>

Date: Tuesday, June 30, 2015 9:35 AM EST

To: Jennifer Dalton <jennydalton431@gmail.com>

Subject: Registration Reminder

Intercontinental Geneve
July 6—July 16, 2015

Dear Valued Guest:

We are looking forward to welcoming you to the 11th Annual Medical Coding Conference in Geneva, Switzerland.

You are registered for:

Full Conference (Presenter)

This package includes:

One (1) Adult—Standard Room with Balcony

Breakfast

Special Meals (Opening Luncheon, Closing Banquet)

Arriving: Monday, July 6, 2015

Departing: Friday, July 17, 2015

MOM AND I soon realized we had another problem: her annual conference in Switzerland.

I usually stay home with Dad, but with him missing, I couldn't do that. Kate was the obvious second choice, but her mother's due date was right in the middle of the trip. Mom couldn't cancel without risking her job, and with Dad gone, that didn't seem like a good idea.

Over dinner, Mom ran through the options. I could stay with another friend, Sophie or Madison or Emily. But they weren't as close friends as Kate. The idea of talking with them about my dad made me feel sick to my stomach. Mom said I could go with her, but I had tried that one year. The hotel pool was fun for about two days and then I had ten more days of drinking hot soda without ice. Besides, what if Dad came home and we were gone? Every suggestion Mom came up with made me feel worse. Finally, I pushed my plate away and ran to my room.

I started looking through all my old emails from Dad. There had to be some clue, right? Some inkling of what he wanted to "think over." I think I found it—or at least I thought I did—in a message from about a month before.

From: Jeffery Dalton <jeffdalton327@gmail.com>

Subject: Road Trip with your Dad?

Date: Monday, May 28, 2015 11:03 AM EST

To: Claudia Dalton <claudiadalton195@gmail.com>

Hey Claudia,

When school's out, why don't we drive up to Papa's for a visit, just you and me. Last time I was there I found some old home movies I wanted to show you. Maybe we could do a few puzzles too. What do you think? Could be a fun father-daughter trip!

Love,

Dad

MY HEART DROPPED when I saw his message. I'd completely forgotten about it. In fact, I remembered being a little annoyed when I'd received it. It was kind of weird. We could watch movies and do puzzles at home. And besides, when school was out, I was looking forward to hanging out with Kate and my other friends at the pool.

So I hadn't responded to the email. Dad had asked me about it at dinner a few days later when Mom was working late, but I guess my lack of enthusiasm must have shown on my face, because he said, "Oh, don't worry about it! We'll do it another time." And he'd never mentioned it again.

I felt so guilty. Why hadn't I agreed to spend one weekend doing what my father had wanted? Why hadn't I thought about my grandfather? Worst of all, I couldn't shake the thought that if I *had* agreed to Dad's plan, maybe he wouldn't have disappeared.

And that's when I came up with the idea.

Claudia Dalton's Cell Phone | Tuesday, June 30, 2015, 3:15 p.m.

Papa: You want to stay with me while your mother goes to Switzerland?

Claudia: Yeah!

Papa: Claudia, your grandmother just died. I'm not sure I'm ready to—

Claudia: I'm a really easy guest.

Papa: I don't know.

Claudia: I've thought it through. We could watch the movies Dad left at your place. And I could keep you company and—

Papa: Claudia, I'm not sure I'm up to company right now. It'd be great to see you, but—

GOT THE HINT—he didn't want me to visit—but I decided to pretend I didn't understand.

Because, truthfully, I was desperate. Once I found the old email from Dad, I knew I *had* to go stay with Papa. I had to go see those home movies. I had to believe they'd give me a clue to why he'd left.

Anyway, I kept arguing. Mom eventually joined in the call. She liked the idea. Thought it would be good for Papa too. And finally, together, we wore him down.

[RECORDING BEGINS]

Lily, you're not going to believe this. Somehow, Claudia talked me into letting her stay with me while her mother goes to Switzerland.

I'm not sure why I agreed. Dr. Larkin said I should shake things up a bit. I don't know, maybe it will be good for me. It's only for two weeks. Claudia was very insistent, and the house *is* too quiet with you gone. Still, I'm a little nervous. What do I know about twelve-year-old girls?!

[RECORDING ENDS]

Claudia Dalton's Cell Phone | Wednesday, July 1, 2015, 12:47 p.m.

KATE

You're going to go stay with your grandfather?

Yeah

But I wanted you to stay with us

My mom says two 12 year olds and a newborn are too much for your family to handle

This baby is ruining my life already
So when are you leaving?

Friday

Friday?!

Mom's flying out on Sunday
She wants to go see the fireworks on Saturday
Papa lives in Alexandria, right outside Washington, DC

That's almost two hours from Richmond!

It's a lot closer than Switzerland if Dad comes back

But Claudia!
You were supposed to take the babysitting/infant care class with me

Oh, that's right!

It starts Monday
We already paid for it

I'm so sorry!
But you can still go

You know I hate doing stuff like that alone!
I need you there!

I'm really sorry, Kate
But what am I supposed to do?!
It was my grandfather or Switzerland!

It's okay
Not your fault
Not like you wanted your dad to disappear

No

And my mom was stressing about
what she would say if your mom asked

Is your mom doing okay?

I guess
She's tired all the time
Says it's a lot harder being pregnant at 42
than it was at 30
She'll be relieved you can go stay with family

I'll miss you

Miss you too
Come over for one last afternoon at the pool?

Yes!

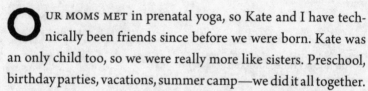

OUR MOMS MET in prenatal yoga, so Kate and I have technically been friends since before we were born. Kate was an only child too, so we were really more like sisters. Preschool, birthday parties, vacations, summer camp—we did it all together.

Kate's parents had always wanted another baby, but after a couple of miscarriages, it seemed like they'd pretty much given up. Sometimes they'd joke about me being their second kid. And then, boom, her mom ended up pregnant at forty-two!

Her mom had been pretty sick, and had about a bazillion doctor's appointments. Kate's parents were already really busy. None of us could quite figure out how they were going to work a new baby into their schedule, even with a full-time nanny.

I don't know why I didn't tell Kate about the videotapes. Maybe it seemed like a long shot, even to me. I felt bad about letting her down, but I didn't see any other choice.

From: Claudia Dalton <claudiadalton195@gmail.com>

Date: Thursday, July 2, 2015 11:03 AM EST

To: Jeffery Dalton <jeffdalton327@gmail.com>

Subject: Going to Papa's House

Dear Dad,

You've been gone almost a week now and I still have no idea why you left. It almost hurts more, knowing you left us on purpose. If you'd been murdered by a serial killer, at least that wouldn't have been your fault.

Anyway, I guess you forgot Mom is going to present at that big insurance conference in Switzerland next week. Remember?! She goes every year. I'm going to go stay with Papa for the next two weeks. Because I found the email you sent me. About the movies. I'll watch them. I promise.

It's going to be strange to visit Papa without Nana. Do you remember the last time we saw her? We did that jungle puzzle with her, the one with all the animals—the tiger, giraffe, kangaroo—drinking at the edge of the river. Papa kept complaining, "Those animals don't even live on the same continent!"

But Nana thought the colors were beautiful. I did the parrot first, and the zebras were pretty easy too, but all those green leaves looked exactly the same. I thought we were never going to finish. But we did, in the end. I'm glad we didn't give up. That was the last puzzle we ever did with her.

Please come home.

Love, Claudia

YOUR TRIP TO:

ALEXANDRIA, VA

1 HR 38 MIN

104 miles

Driving time based on traffic as of 12:03 PM on July 3, 2015.

Current Traffic: Moderate

- Turn right onto E Broad St
- Merge onto I-95 N toward Washington
- Take US-1 exit 177B on the left toward Alexandria
- Turn right onto Duke St
- Turn right onto Calahan Dr
- Turn left onto Maple St
- Turn right onto Poplar Ln
  Your destination will be on the right.

4821 Poplar Lane
Alexandria, VA

Claudia Dalton's Cell Phone | Friday, July 3, 2015, 8:27 p.m.

TEXT MESSAGE

KATE

Made it to Papa's

Good

What you doing?

Helping Dad paint the nursery

Your dad is painting?

Well, he's not home yet
I'm getting things ready
He'll be here soon

What color?

Buttercup yellow

Nice

Any word from your dad?

No

Sorry

I better go
Gonna watch some old home
movies with Papa and Mom

Have fun!

Thanks
Good luck painting!

47

INT. PAPA'S KITCHEN—DAY

Claudia is eight years old. She wears flowered pajamas and sits at the kitchen island, doing a puzzle with Nana. Her grandmother's hair is gray and matches the trim on her fluffy pink robe. There are lines on her face, but her eyes are bright and sharp as she searches for pieces.

Mom sips a mug of coffee; Dad pours himself a cup of tea. It's early morning. Dad sits down on a stool next to Claudia.

DAD

What puzzle are you doing?

CLAUDIA

"Pirates and Buried Treasure."

DAD

Can I help?

CLAUDIA

Sure.

He picks up a piece and starts working. After a moment, Claudia sighs.

CLAUDIA (CONT'D)

I wish I could find a buried treasure. That'd be so exciting!

NANA

Well, I don't know about treasure, but there is a time capsule in our backyard.

CLAUDIA

Really?!

NANA

Yes, your father buried it one summer. I think
he was about thirteen. Never told anyone where
it was.

Claudia turns to her father, grinning.

CLAUDIA

Where is it?

Her dad keeps his eyes firmly on the puzzle.

DAD

Oh, I don't remember.

Her mom stirs in her cream.

MOM

Well, what's in it?

DAD

Nothing.

MOM

There's got to be something.

PAPA (O.S.)

Probably a mixtape he made for some girl.

Nana and Mom laugh.

> CLAUDIA
>
> Look! Daddy's blushing.

> MOM
>
> Then it must be true!

Dad blushes furiously and keeps working on the puzzle.

———

INT. RESTAURANT—NIGHT
Claudia is younger here, maybe five years old. She's wearing an American flag T-shirt and has stars painted on her cheeks. The whole family is out to dinner, sitting in a big booth.

> NANA
>
> Put that camera away.

> CLAUDIA
>
> Papa said I could sing him a song. He's gonna tape it.

> NANA
>
> After dinner, sweetie.

A very pretty young waitress, wearing a red, white, and blue blouse, comes up to the table and smiles at Claudia's dad.

> WAITRESS
>
> What can I get you, sir?

———

INT. RESTAURANT—LATER

Everyone's done eating. Claudia, Nana, and Papa scoot out one side of the booth.

                    CLAUDIA

    Can I sing now?!

                    PAPA (O.S.)

    Go for it!

Claudia launches into her song.

                    CLAUDIA

    "O, say can you see! By the dawn's early . . ."

Mom and Dad pick up the boxes of leftovers.

                    MOM

    That waitress was cute.

                    DAD

    Really? I didn't notice.

She leans over and gives him a kiss.

                    MOM

    Aren't you a sweetie.

Dad smiles, but he's focused on Claudia, who is still singing, loudly and dramatically.

CLAUDIA

". . . banner yet wave. O'er the land of the free, and the home of the brave!"

NANA

Yay! Great job.

CLAUDIA

Daddy taught me. Is it time for sparklers?!

From: Claudia Dalton <claudiadalton195@gmail.com>

Date: Friday, July 3, 2015 11:15 PM EST

To: Jeffery Dalton <jeffdalton327@gmail.com>

Subject: In Alexandria now . . .

Dear Dad,

Papa was waiting for us on the front porch when we pulled up. He gave Mom and me a big hug, and if he looked a little thinner than he had at Nana's funeral, we all pretended not to notice.

I'm staying in your old room, like I always do. That mattress is so lumpy. And why didn't Nana ever take down your *Star Wars* posters? Or replace the faded Charlie Brown sheets? The house always looks exactly the same, down to the photo of you when you were twelve on the coffee table.

After dinner, I talked Mom and Papa into watching some of our old movies. In the first, I was about eight, and Nana was talking about when you buried a time capsule in the backyard. Do you remember that conversation? I didn't until we watched it. I spent the rest of that weekend digging holes in Nana and Papa's backyard, but I never found a thing.

That was fun. I'd still like to hear that mixtape.

The second was the 4th of July, the year you taught me "The Star-Spangled Banner" and I wouldn't stop singing it. Do you remember?

It was fun watching the videos, but I have to admit, I don't know why you wanted me to see them. It's just . . . normal stuff. Now it's late, and I can't sleep, and you probably aren't reading these messages anyway. But just in case you are, please come home.

Love, Claudia

A Hometown CELEBRATION

Maury School Playground
Russell Road
Alexandria, VA

**Saturday, July 4, 2015
9:00 a.m. – 1:00 p.m.**

Hot dogs, hamburgers, soft drinks,
popcorn, snow cones.

Watermelon-eating contest!

Relay races!

Baby beauty contest!

Dunking booth!

Bike-decorating contest!

For more information, contact Tisha Walters at 703-555-7831

I DIDN'T REALLY WANT to go to the celebration at the local elementary school, but Mom insisted. The event was all babies and decorated bikes, dunking booths and cakewalks. I watched all the happy families strolling around, eating cotton candy and running relay races, and it made me a little sad. We used to be one of those families. With Dad gone—what were we now?

Mom was quieter than usual. I guess the dogs with ribbons and snow cones weren't enough to cheer her up. We came home after about an hour, bringing Papa a hamburger for lunch, and sat down to watch some more home movies.

INT. AIR AND SPACE MUSEUM—DAY

Six-year-old Claudia hangs on the railing, staring at something. She wears her hair in pigtails and has a chocolate ice cream stain on her shirt. The camera pulls out to reveal a huge spacecraft. Her dad stares with her.

DAD

Pretty amazing, isn't it?!

CLAUDIA

Yeah.

DAD

Humans lived in orbit in a craft just like this one.
Skylab was the very first space station.

CLAUDIA

Wow!

Dad bends down so he's at Claudia's level and whispers in her ear.

DAD

What if we go home and build our very own space
station?

Claudia inhales in excitement.

CLAUDIA

Can we do that?!

DAD

I don't see why not. All we need is a big box.

_____

EXT. PAPA'S BACKYARD—DAY

An old refrigerator box, aka the "space station," sits under the cherry tree in the backyard. It has *USA* painted on one side. Claudia stands next to a picnic table, studying it, hands on her tiny hips.

Dad comes out the back door, carrying a roll of aluminum foil.

DAD

Here it is! The foil we need to protect us from the sun.

He pulls a huge piece off the roll and lays it flat on the picnic table.

CLAUDIA

But it's supposed to be orange.

Dad glances at the picnic table. There's a basket of art supplies, markers, paints, and brushes.

DAD

We can paint it!

He hands a cup to Claudia and squeezes in a little red and a little yellow paint. He hands her a Popsicle stick. She grins and stirs it as carefully as if it were a pot of gold.

———

EXT. MERRY-GO-ROUND—DAY

There's a merry-go-round at a county fair. Dad sits on a huge white horse. Claudia is tiny, not yet three, and sits in front of him, a safety belt wrapped around her waist. She's clutching the pole with her little hands and looks terrified.

PAPA (O.S.)

She's too little.

NANA (O.S.)
She's with her dad. She'll be okay!

The bell rings and the ride starts. Dad and Claudia circle around, away from the camera.

A moment later, they come back around, both grinning. The wind is blowing Claudia's hair into her eyes. She waves at the camera.

THE HOME MOVIES gave me no hint where Dad might have gone, and seeing us all so happy just made me miss him more. Still, Mom and I kept watching, all afternoon. Papa hovered in the doorway. Mom told him to come sit on the couch at least three times. He insisted he was going to go lie down for a bit. But he never left.

EXT. PAPA'S BACKYARD—DAY

Seven-year-old Claudia wears a lavender dress and patent leather shoes with white lacy socks. She's clutching an Easter basket. Dad holds out a small blue plastic egg.

DAD

There are clues inside each one.

Claudia wrestles the blue egg open. She pulls out a slip of paper.

CLAUDIA

"I grow small red fruit."

She looks at Dad and smiles.

CLAUDIA (CONT'D)

The cherry tree!

———

EXT. PAPA'S BACKYARD—LATER

Claudia climbs a branch of the cherry tree, moving toward a yellow plastic egg.

PAPA (O.S.)

She's going to get her dress dirty.

NANA

Don't be silly, dear. That's what washing machines are for.

Claudia retrieves the egg and sits back on a branch to open it.

CLAUDIA

"Little animals swim in me." The fish pond!

_____

EXT. PAPA'S BACKYARD—LATER

Claudia stands by the edge of the tiny pool. There are orange gold-
fish swimming in the murky water. At the bottom of the pool is a
green egg. She reaches in.

MOM

You made a whole treasure hunt?

Dad nods. Nana smiles.

NANA

He liked to do that as a kid too.

Mom gives him a hug.

MOM

What a great idea!

Claudia squeals and holds up the green egg.

DAD

Only two more clues until the chocolate bunny!

_____

EXT. BEACH PARK—DAY

At the bottom of a hill is a swing set and a metal jungle gym, painted
red and yellow. Claudia is about nine and hangs upside down from

one of the monkey bars, her little T-shirt tucked into her shorts so it doesn't fall onto her face.

> CLAUDIA
>
> Daddy! Come play too.

Her father grabs the bar next to Claudia and hangs for a moment. Then he swings his legs up and wraps his knees around the bars.

> PAPA (O.S.)
>
> Careful, Jeff.

Dad hangs upside down like his daughter. But he's so tall, his hands reach the mulch on the ground beneath them. Claudia, still upside down next to her father, laughs and laughs.

EXT. POOL—DAY

Claudia is ten now and wears a one-piece swimsuit covered with watermelons, pineapples, and strawberries. Nana is in the pool, swimming laps. A group of other kids, some about Claudia's age, gather by the snack bar, eating ice cream. Claudia sits on a lawn chair, wrapped in a towel, listening to her father read a book.

> DAD
>
> "The sheep an inch and half, more or less: their geese about the bigness of a sparrow, and so the several gradations downwards till you come to the smallest, which to my sight, were almost invisible; but nature has adapted the eyes of the Lilliputians to all objects proper for their view."

The lifeguard blows a whistle. Nana gets out of the pool and starts to dry off.

NANA

Break is over now. You can go back in the pool if you want.

Claudia glances at her grandmother and then back at her father.

CLAUDIA

Can we finish this chaper of *Gulliver's Travels* first?

Dad grins.

WHEN WE WERE done watching the home movies, it was time to go watch the fireworks. But even though they were beautiful, I couldn't concentrate. I'd done what my father had asked, and now I was even more confused. The videos had reminded me of how much fun we'd had together. I'd always thought he was a great dad, but now he was also the jerk who had left without an explanation. Which one was my real father?

Walter Dalton's Cell Phone | Saturday, July 4, 2015, 11:02 p.m.

[RECORDING BEGINS]

Lily, it's late. We just got home from the fireworks. But I had a hard time focusing on them, because, well, I spent all afternoon watching home movies with Jenny and Claudia.

Jeff was such a good dad. He did so much with Claudia. Sometimes I think I could have been a better father to him, could have done more with him and—

Well, it doesn't matter now. Jenny is leaving tomorrow and then Claudia and I will be on our own. Maybe these two weeks are an opportunity to . . . I don't know. Better get some rest.

[RECORDING ENDS]

Claudia Dalton's Cell Phone | Sunday, July 5, 2015, 4:16 p.m.

Mom: At my gate.

Claudia: Great. Have a good trip!

Mom: Thanks. I hope you and Papa have a—

Claudia: Mom?

Mom: What?

Claudia: Is it my fault Dad left?

Mom: Why would it be your fault?

Claudia: I never told you, but . . . Dad asked me to watch those home movies with him about a month ago and I said no.

Mom: Oh, Claudia! Why didn't you say something? Is that why you wanted to see them?

Claudia: Yeah. I felt so bad I'd blown him off.

Mom: Sweetie, you're almost thirteen! Of course you don't want to hang out with your dad all the time.

Claudia: But Nana died and I knew he was sad about that. And if I had just spent a little time with him, maybe he would still be—

Mom: Claudia, listen to me. I don't know why he left. But I'm one hundred percent certain it had nothing to do with you.

Claudia: Really?

Mom: Yes.

[NOISE IN THE BACKGROUND]

Mom: My plane is boarding. I have to go. Love you, sweetie.

Claudia: I love you too, Mom.

Mom: We'll find him, Claudia. He'll come home. We just need to be patient. And it's not your fault!

I KNEW MOM WAS was trying to make me feel better. But I didn't really believe her. Dad had been gone for ten days—I was tired of being patient.

Dinner with Papa was quiet and awkward. I hadn't realized how much Mom talked. We ate sandwiches and chips and didn't speak. I put my dishes in the dishwasher and went to Dad's room as soon as I was done.

It wasn't even late, but I brushed my teeth and climbed into the lumpy bed. What had I been thinking? Why in the world had I thought watching old movies would help? I felt so stupid. I wished I had gotten on the plane with Mom. I wished I had stayed with a friend or gone to camp or . . . I wished I were anywhere except here, with Papa. We had nothing in common, nothing to talk about.

I missed Nana, her jokes and her hugs and how she always had a puzzle on the table. I'd thought staying with Papa would be better than being at home, where every time I turned a corner, I half expected to run into my father. But no. At Papa's, I was reminded that my grandmother was gone, too.

I cried myself to sleep, thinking I would always be where I was, stuck, not knowing what to do.

Of course, the next day when Papa got the mail, I received a letter and everything started to change.

Monday, July 6, 2015, 12:45 p.m.

Item #1: Flyer printed on light blue paper: Family Fun Night at
         the National Air and Space Museum
Item #2: Ad for Mama's Pizza Palace: Wednesday night is half-off!
Item #3: Letter addressed to:

Claudia Dalton
c/o Walter Dalton
4821 Poplar Lane
Alexandria, VA 22301

Postmark:
7/2/15
NYC

Inside is one puzzle piece.
On the picture side is something shiny and gold.
On the back are four words:

*Find the
time capsule*

PART 2
The Puzzle

Jeff's Puzzles

1. Trucks and Cars (100)
2. Flowers for Grandma (50)
3. Neuschwanstein (1500)
4. Leaping Lizards (90)
5. The Periodic Table (1000)
6. Elephants of the Wild (500)
7. Gold Rush (300)
8. Jack and the Beanstalk (100)
9. Coffee and Muffins (500)
10. On the Farm (250)
11. Days of the Week (20)
12. King of the Savanna (500)
13. Popular Penguins (250)
14. Months of the Year (50)
15. Jack and the Beanstalk (500)
16. Treasure Chest (300)
17. Little Llamas (50)
18. Dumbo Gets a Feather (75)
19. The Washington Monument (500)
20. The Giant of the Deep (250)
21. The White House (500)
22. David and Goliath (2000)
23. Piles of Puppies (500)
24. Midas's Touch (100)
25. Rocks & Gems (100)
26. Lemonade Stand (500)
27. Ketchup & Kittens (300)
28. Seashells by the Seashore (500)
29. Milk and Cookies (100)
30. Apple Orchard (500)
31. Learn Your Letters (26)
32. Firemen at Work (100)
33. Here Comes Peter Cottontail (300)
34. The Titans (1000)
35. The Star-Spangled Banner (500)
36. Garbage Truck (50)
37. The County Fair (300)
38. Real Rabbits (300)
39. Ice Cream (100)
40. United States (50)
41. *Star Wars*: Stormtroopers Stop the Landspeeder (140)

42. Candy Bars (100)

43. Valentine Villains (200)

44. Linderhof (500)

45. The World (100)

46. Paul Bunyan (750)

47. Soccer Balls (400)

48. Pirates and Buried Treasure (300)

49. Knights of the Round Table (250)

50. The Planets (100)

51. T-Rex on the Loose (150)

52. Jack-o'-lanterns (500)

53. *Gulliver's Travels* (300)

54. Edible Alphabet (50)

55. Zebra Stripes (1000)

56. Popsicles (300)

57. Steam Engines (1000)

58. O Tannenbaum (500)

59. Marvelous Monkeys (1500)

60. Saturn and Its Rings (200)

61. The Dollhouse (500)

62. Basketballs (300)

63. *The Wizard of Oz*: Follow the Yellow Brick Road (200)

64. River in the Jungle (500)

65. Roses (100)

66. Lilies (100)

67. Stegosaurus and Friends (75)

68. The Cursed Jewel (200)

69. Daisies (100)

70. Virginia (50)

71. The Smithsonian Castle (1000)

72. Orbiting Earth (1000)

73. The Grand Tetons (500)

74. The Eiffel Tower (500)

75. Andre the Giant: *The Princess Bride* (1000)

76. Fire Truck (350)

77. Irish Lasses (200)

78. Old Faithful (500)

79. Luscious Lips (350)

80. Golden Gate Bridge (500)

81. Beach Balls (50)

82. Gigantic Giraffes (1500)

83. The Golden Egg (300)

84. The Evening Sky (1000)

85. Santa's Reindeer (500)

86. Mickey & Minnie (50)

From: Claudia Dalton <claudiadalton195@gmail.com>
Date: Monday, July 6, 2015 1:15 PM EST
To: Jeffery Dalton <jeffdalton327@gmail.com>
Subject: The puzzle piece!!

Dear Dad,

You ARE reading these emails!!

As soon as I got the piece, I ran up to the attic to look at the two bookshelves completely filled with all the old puzzles. But I don't understand! The piece you sent has a blob of something golden on the front. But what does that mean? There are over a hundred puzzles on the bookshelves in the attic. And about half the puzzles have something golden on them. I found the list taped to the side of the first bookshelf, but . . . how do I know which puzzle to do?

Love, Claudia

PS. Is this like those treasure hunts you used to write for me when I was little? If I find the time capsule, will you come home?

PPS. I think you will. Because there was always a prize at the end.

PPPS. See you soon!

Claudia Dalton's Cell Phone | Monday, July 6, 2015, 4:05 p.m.

PHONE TRANSCRIPT

Claudia: Hi, Mom.

Mom: Hi, sweetie. I just got back to my hotel and—

Claudia: Mom, I heard from Dad!

Mom: What?! Did he call or—

Claudia: No, no. He sent me a puzzle piece.

Mom: A puzzle piece?

Claudia: Yeah.

Mom: Why?

Claudia: I told you how I've been sending him emails, right?

Mom: Yes.

Claudia: Well, I didn't think he was reading them. But he is!

Mom: How do you know?

Claudia: Because he knew I was at Papa's. And I mentioned something about that old mixtape he buried in the backyard. And then he sent me a puzzle piece and wrote on the back "Find the time capsule."

Mom: He sent you a puzzle piece?

Claudia: Yes!

Mom: [SILENCE]

Claudia: Say something.

Mom: I don't know what to say.

Claudia: What do you think this means?

Mom: I don't know, sweetie.

Claudia: I think it means if I find the time capsule, he'll come home.

Mom: Oh, Claudia. Did he say that?

Claudia: Well, not exactly, but . . .

Mom: I think your dad is thinking about you. I'm not sure you should read much more—

Claudia: Why are you being so mean?

Mom: I'm not being mean. I'm being realistic.

Claudia: I'm going to find the time capsule and I'm going to find Dad!

Mom: Okay, okay. Look, I'm exhausted, I barely slept on the plane last night. Let's talk about this tomorrow.

Claudia: Fine.

Mom: I love you, sweetie.

Claudia: Yeah. Love you too.

KATE

He sent you a puzzle piece?
That's kind of a weird thing to do
If you want to tell someone something,
send a letter or a text or call
But a puzzle piece?

> I thought you'd be excited for me

I am excited
It's just odd

> You sound like my mother

Sorry, just kind of tired
Mom and I were up late painting
the nursery last night

> Your dad didn't . . .

No

> Sorry

I don't want to talk about it

> Okay
> Hey, didn't you have your
> first baby care class today?

Yup

> And?

Kinda awful

75

They made us play that game where you have to go around in a circle repeating everyone's name

You hate that one

Yup
It's all your fault!

I'm sorry 🙁
Did you learn anything?

Yes. First three months after a baby is born is sometimes called the 4th trimester
Basically, they just eat, poop, sleep, and cry
Sounds great, doesn't it?

Haha
Wish I were there

I GOTTA ADMIT, I was a little hurt that Mom and Kate weren't more enthusiastic. I mean, I knew it sounded crazy, but now I had something to do!

That afternoon, I worked three puzzles with gold: "The Golden Egg," "Midas's Touch," and "Pirates and Buried Treasure." That was the one from the video! I figured that had to be it, but the piece didn't fit in any of them.

I took the list of puzzles down from the bookshelf in the attic and carefully checked off the ones I had done. Three down. One hundred two to go.

[RECORDING BEGINS]

Lily, now he's sending puzzle pieces. I don't know what to think. Claudia's so excited. She spent all afternoon doing puzzles. I wanted to help her, but I'm just not good at jigsaws. You were always begging me to try. Said I'd get better with practice. I should have done a few more puzzles with you.

Dinner was so quiet again. Wish I could think of something to say. I've invited the new neighbors over tomorrow night. I'm pretty sure they have a kid Claudia's age. Maybe if she has a friend, things won't be so awkward.

I miss you, Lily. You were the one who knew how to make conversation. "Claudia, tell us about sixth grade! Is Kate in your class this year?" Or "Walter's team won the bowling league championship last week. Want to see his trophy?" You were the one who brought us together. Without you, it's like we're just two strangers sharing a table at a crowded coffee shop.

[RECORDING ENDS]

GIANT FOOD
425 E. Monroe Avenue
Alexandria, VA 22301
Store Telephone: (703) 555-8149

Store #752   7/7/15   9:45 AM

GROCERY
GROUND BEEF, 80%   5.99
HAMBURGER BUNS   1.99
   BONUS BUY SAVINGS   0.15-
   PRICE YOU PAY   1.84
KETCHUP   1.79
MUSTARD   2.49
CORN ON THE COB   1.99
BAKED BEANS   1.69

Total Before Savings   15.94
Your Savings   0.15
Total After Savings   15.79
TAX   0.39
**BALANCE   16.18

****
Payment Type: CREDIT
Card: **** **** **** 6342
Payment Amt: $16.18

From: Claudia Dalton <claudiadalton195@gmail.com>
Date: Tuesday, July 7, 2015 7:49 PM EST
To: Jeffery Dalton <jeffdalton327@gmail.com>
Subject: Cookout

Dear Dad,

Papa invited the neighbors over for a cookout this afternoon. They were nice enough, I guess. The man and the woman are both lawyers. They have a little baby and a boy my age. They made us sit next to each other, like we were going to be friends because, *gasp,* we are both going into 7th grade! But my "new best friend" just spent the whole evening filming stuff with this video camera. Apparently, he's taking some documentary film class that involves recording people's "real-life stories." But who wants to watch someone flip hamburgers?!

Anyway, it felt really weird to be cooking out at Papa's. I think the last time we did was about a year ago. You were the grillmeister, and I was helping, but somehow, we still burned the hot dogs. Nana said she liked them that way.

About a month after that, the doctor figured out why Nana had been tired so much. That didn't cause it, right? I mean, eating too much processed meat has been linked to a higher risk of cancer. But her cancer didn't come from the one burnt hot dog I served her, right?

I know it didn't. Just . . . cooking out made me think about it. Papa only bought burgers this time, but hot dogs were Nana's favorite. I wonder if Papa was thinking about that too.

Was there something I did to make you leave? Are you mad we stopped doing stuff together? I'm sorry, but I don't understand what you're trying to tell me. Why do I need to find the time capsule? Please send another clue.

Love, Claudia

KATE

How was class?

A little less awful today
Learned how to swaddle a baby

What's that?

Wrap them tight in a big blanket so they
don't flail around and wake themselves up
Had to practice on a doll

And?

The doll didn't complain

Haha

What you up to?

We had a cookout with the neighbors

Wow, quite the social life with old gramps

Yeah
It's kind of awkward when
it's just Papa and me
I think it was a friend setup.
The family has a son our age

Ooooh!!

Haha

Was he cute?

I guess

That means yes

. . .

LUIS

Hi. This is Luis from across the street

KATE

OMG, he just texted me!!!

What?????

LUIS

Your grandpa gave my mom your number

KATE

What do I say?

What did he say?

"Hi. This is Luis from across the street. Your grandpa gave my mom your number"

Say hi

No

Do it!!

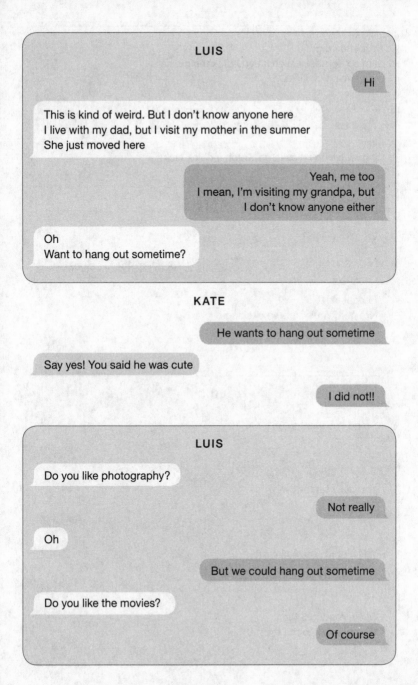

83

We should go
I'm so bored, I'll even let you pick the movie
Just no chick flicks

Haha

JK
I'm so bored I'd even go watch a chick flick

KATE

What'd he say?

He wants to go to the movies sometime

Eeeeekkkk!!
Not fair!! Your life is so exciting

Kate!!

LUIS

So do you want to go?

Sure

You busy tomorrow?

Tomorrow?

You already have plans?

No

Okay. Around 3 then
We can walk to the theater

Okay

Cool. See you then

KATE

We're going to the movies tomorrow!

Eeeeekk!!
What does he look like?

He's totally out of my league
Like boy-band pretty

Take a selfie at the movies
Are you gonna kiss him?

Kate!

Sorry. Just glad something good happened

Yeah. Guess I am too
Is it bad to be happy about something
even though my father's gone?

Of course not

It feels wrong

Shut up and stop worrying
And call me when you get home

I WAS SUPER EXCITED about being invited to the movies. I would tell you how cute Luis is, but he's actually ended up helping me with a lot of the things in this binder, and the comment about him being "boy-band pretty" is already embarrassing enough.

But I didn't tell Mom about Luis when she called. I was still hurt she wasn't more excited about the puzzle. I didn't want her to be "realistic" about the movies too.

FANDANGO

Your purchase is complete! This page is your Print at Home ticket.

With this printed page, go directly to the ticket-taker.

New! Send Mobile Ticket to my mobile device, too.

2 matinee ticket(s) to:

ZOMBIES AND EXPLOSIONS 4

Date: **Wednesday, July 8, 2015**

AMC Hoffman Center 22

Auditorium: 6

Time: 3:35 PM

206 Swamp Fox Rd.

Alexandria, VA 22314

CONFIRMATION NUMBER: A05620R789J

Kate: Hello?

Claudia: It. Was. Awful!

Kate: Oh no. What happened?

Claudia: First of all, it was pouring rain, so his mom had to give us a ride.

Kate: Awkward!

Claudia: Yup. And yesterday he said I could pick the movie. But when we arrived at the theater, it turned out he had already bought tickets for *Zombies and Explosions 4*.

Kate: But you hate zombie movies!

Claudia: I know.

Kate: Did you say something?

Claudia: No, I didn't know what to say! Then he was hungry, and since he'd paid for the tickets, I said I'd get the popcorn. He ordered the biggest popcorn there was *and* a large soda. It cost more than the tickets!

Kate: Yeah, that's how theaters make their money.

Claudia: Whatever. Anyway, the movie starts. You know how I am in horror movies?

Kate: Yeah, you always jump.

Claudia: Yup.

Kate: Oh no.

Claudia: The first zombie lurches out of one of the exploding cars and I jump.

Kate: Oh no.

Claudia: Luis picks that exact moment to take a sip of his soda. And my jumping startles him.

Kate: Oh no.

Claudia: So he flinches and spills his soda all over me!

Kate: Okay, I know I shouldn't laugh but . . . hahahahahahaha-hahahaha!

Claudia: Shut up. We had to leave in the middle of the movie. Then, while I was shaking the soda and ice cubes off my T-shirt, the puzzle piece from my dad falls out of my pocket!

Kate: You were carrying it around with you?

Claudia: I don't want to lose it! It's the only clue I have. But of course, Luis, trying to be helpful, picked it up and wanted to know why I had a puzzle piece in my pocket.

Kate: What'd you say?

Claudia: I just told him the truth.

Kate: What did he say?

Claudia: He thought it was the coolest thing ever. Started going on and on about how he should have brought his camera.

Kate: His camera?

Claudia: His dad bought him a semi-pro camera and now his goal is to spend the summer filming "real-life stories."

Kate: That's kinda cool.

Claudia: Not when you're covered in soda.

Kate: Oh no. What happened?

Claudia: He wanted to go home so I could retell him the story about the puzzle piece and he could film it this time.

Kate: What did you say?

Claudia: I started yelling at him to get me a paper towel. Then he ran to the bathroom and came back with a roll of toilet paper. When I tried to use it to dry off my T-shirt, it disintegrated and left little bits of paper everywhere. So he ran back to the bathroom, but they were out of paper towels, and it sort of went downhill from there.

Kate: Geez.

Claudia: I can't believe I was covered in soda and he was going on and on about filming me telling my story. So rude!

Kate: Hmm.

Claudia: You don't think so?!

Kate: He thought you were interesting enough to interview. I think I might be flattered.

Claudia: Really?

Kate: Yeah. It's nice when people want to spend time with you.

Claudia: Oh. Are you okay, Kate?

Kate: I had to eat dinner alone all this week.

Claudia: I'm sorry. Did you say anything—

Kate: My mom keeps saying, "I have to wrap up this project before I go on maternity leave." And my dad, well, if he responds to my texts, which he doesn't always do, it's always one word. Sure. OK. Later. Sorry.

Claudia: Geez, Kate. That's awful.

Kate: If they are like this now, what's it going to be like when the baby comes?!

Claudia: You're always welcome at our house for dinner.

Kate: You're not here!

Claudia: I know. I'm sorry.

Kate: It's okay.

Claudia: Don't be too jealous. I totally overreacted at the movies, didn't I?

Kate: Maybe a little.

Claudia: He's never going to talk to me again!

Kate: I thought you didn't like him anyway.

Claudia: Shut up.

Kate: I'm sorry it wasn't more fun.

Claudia: Thanks. I'm sorry you're feeling lonely. How's the class going?

Kate: Today we covered diapers and burping techniques.

Claudia: That's a thing?

Kate: Apparently.

Claudia: Miss you.

Kate: Miss you too.

Claudia Dalton's Cell Phone | Wednesday, July 8, 2015, 7:34 p.m.

Claudia: Hello?

Luis: I know what it is!

Claudia: What?

Luis: The puzzle piece. It's C-3PO's head!

Claudia: What?!

Luis: The puzzle piece you had in your pocket. The one from your dad. I just realized why it looks familiar. It's C-3PO! The droid from *Star Wars*.

Claudia: Oh yeah! My dad was a big *Star Wars* fan.

Luis: Is there a *Star Wars* puzzle on the list?

Claudia: Let me check. Call you back in a minute.

———

7:41 p.m.

Claudia: Yes! There is! It's called "*Star Wars*: Stormtroopers Stop the Landspeeder."

Luis: Cool! How many pieces?

Claudia: Only 140. There's an old VHS copy of the movie in the box too.

Luis: We gotta do it tonight.

Claudia: Tonight?

Luis: Can I come over? Can I bring my camera?!

Claudia: Um, yeah, sure, I guess.

Luis: Great. See you in five.

INT. PAPA'S KITCHEN—NIGHT

Claudia and Papa are sitting at the island, working the *Star Wars* puzzle. The box shows Luke and Obi-Wan in the landspeeder, with C-3PO and R2-D2 in the back. They are all surrounded by Stormtroopers.

Claudia keeps looking up at the camera.

> CLAUDIA
>
> Why are you always filming things?

> LUIS (O.S.)
>
> I'm taking a class on cinema verité.

> CLAUDIA
>
> What's that?

> LUIS (O.S.)
>
> It's a style of documentary filmmaking. The camera is acknowledged, which means you don't have to pretend it's not there.

> PAPA
>
> It's a French thing, right? Started in the 1960s?

> CLAUDIA
>
> You've heard of this?!

Papa shrugs.

> PAPA
>
> Your grandmother used to drag me to all these weird foreign films.

LUIS (O.S.)

Yeah, it started in France. It's all about finding truth in images and everyday interactions. There's usually not even any voice-over narration.

CLAUDIA

Then how do you know what's going on?

LUIS (O.S.)

You have to figure it out yourself by what you see and hear. As a filmmaker, you really find your story in the editing room and have to piece it all together. It's super cool!

NOTE TO READER

'VE GOT TO be honest with you. When Luis started going on and on about all this "cinema verité" stuff, I did not think it sounded super cool. I thought it sounded super dorky and weird. And a big waste of time. What if you spent hours filming "everyday life" and nothing interesting ever happened?!

I mean, who really wants to watch someone working a puzzle? But I felt bad I'd been rude at the movies and I'd thought about what Kate said about taking it as a compliment if someone wanted to interview you. And Luis had helped find the *Star Wars* puzzle. So I figured I could deal, even if his filming was a little annoying.

INT. PAPA'S KITCHEN—NIGHT

Claudia and Papa are still working on the puzzle.

> LUIS (O.S.)
>
> And so, for this class I'm supposed to film all my
> footage this summer, and then we're going to work on
> editing it in the fall.

> CLAUDIA
>
> Hmm.

Luis steps closer, filming over her shoulder.

> LUIS (O.S.)
>
> Hey, I remember this scene! It's from the original
> movie—right before Obi-Wan uses the Jedi mind trick
> on the Stormtroopers. "These aren't the droids you're
> looking for."

Claudia looks up him and smiles.

> CLAUDIA
>
> Yeah. Dad used to use the Jedi mind trick on me with
> cookies. When there was only one left on the plate,
> he'd wave his hand and say, "You do not want to eat
> this cookie!"

> LUIS (O.S.)
>
> Did it work?

> CLAUDIA
>
> Yeah. I'd laugh so hard, I'd always end up splitting it
> with him.

Luis laughs. Papa smiles too.

                    LUIS (O.S.)
That's awesome.

                    CLAUDIA
There are only a couple of pieces left.

Luis zooms in. One is the gold piece that says "Find the time capsule" on the back. Sure enough, Claudia snaps that piece into
place as C-3PO's head. There's now only one piece missing from
the puzzle, from the side of R2-D2.

But the final piece in Claudia's hand is not blue or white or silver. It's black. Black as night. Darth Vader black, with random
specks of white.

Papa hovers by her side.

                    PAPA
What are you waiting for?

                    CLAUDIA
It's the wrong one. It's not going to fit.

                    LUIS (O.S.)
Try it anyway.

Claudia does. It doesn't fit. She tries it again.

                    CLAUDIA
See?!

She flips it over in frustration. On the back is written: "Entrance
to Skylab."

                    CLAUDIA (CONT'D)
        It says something!

                         PAPA
        Let me see.

He picks up the piece.

                    LUIS (O.S.)
        Hold it up so I can get a better shot.

He zooms in even closer.

                         PAPA
        There's an *R* near the round part here . . .

                        CLAUDIA
        That's called a tab. The empty parts are pockets.

                    LUIS (O.S.)
        "Entrance to Skylab." And the letter *R*. What does
        that mean?

                        CLAUDIA
        I don't know.

                         PAPA
        Skylab?

Claudia picks up her phone and types quickly.

                        CLAUDIA
        It's an old space station from the 1970s.

PAPA

Oh yeah. It's at the museum in the city.

CLAUDIA

From the video! Dad and I made it out of a cardboard
box. Which museum was it?

PAPA

Air and Space.

Claudia puts down her phone.

CLAUDIA

Where'd you put the junk mail?

PAPA

What?

CLAUDIA

Just tell me.

PAPA

In the recycling. With the newspapers. Over there.

He points to a magazine holder in the corner. Claudia rushes over
and starts sorting through it.

LUIS (O.S.)

What are you doing?

CLAUDIA

There was a flyer. Blue. It came the same day as the
puzzle piece.

She's throwing paper everywhere.

                              PAPA
              Claudia, what are you talking . . .

Claudia holds up a blue piece of paper.

                             CLAUDIA
              Family Fun Night. Tomorrow. Six p.m. At the National
              Air and Space Museum. And it's postmarked from
              New York. I thought it was junk, but no. Dad sent this
              too. Look!

Family Fun Night

at the

National Air and Space Museum

Independence Avenue at 6th Street SW
Washington, DC 20560

Come learn about flight, space travel, and more
at the second annual community event.

For all ages
Admission: Free
Thursday, July 9, 2015
6:00–9:00 p.m.

From: Claudia Dalton <claudiadalton195@gmail.com>
Date: Wednesday, July 8, 2015 9:42 PM EST
To: Jeffery Dalton <jeffdalton327@gmail.com>
Subject: Star Wars Puzzle

Dear Dad,

WE FOUND IT!!

The piece you sent was from the puzzle of Luke and Obi-Wan in the landspeeder. We did the puzzle and we found the next piece.

Entrance to Skylab.

I remembered Skylab from our old home movies. But I still didn't know what it meant. Until I realized you sent us another clue—the flyer!

When I saw your message, I got goose bumps. Literally. Luis did too. Oh, I don't think I've told you about him. He's the boy who lives across the street and wants to be a documentary filmmaker. He taped the whole thing and said it was the best footage he's ever gotten.

And of course we're coming to the museum event tomorrow. Papa's going to drive us. 6:00 p.m. You're gonna be there, aren't you?! Remember when we made that cardboard Skylab together?!! It was so much fun.

See you tomorrow!!

Love, Claudia

I WAS TOO EXCITED to sleep, so I told Papa we should watch the old VHS tape of *Star Wars* to celebrate finding the puzzle. Only took me a minute to dust off the VCR in the attic and hook it up to the TV. (Nana saved everything!)

But when we popped in the videotape labeled *Star Wars*, it wasn't what either of us was expecting.

EXT. UPTOWN THEATER—NIGHT

On the street outside the Uptown Theater in Washington, DC. This is an old-style theater, complete with marquee lights. Jeff and Brian, both about twelve years old, stand in a long line. It's the mid-1980s and they're both wearing jean jackets.

> PAPA (O.S.)
> And here, Jeff and Brian are waiting to see *Star Wars* on the big screen for the very first time!

> BRIAN
> My dad actually took me to see it when I was three.

> JEFF
> Do you remember it?

> BRIAN
> No.

Jeff punches Brian's shoulder.

> JEFF
> Then it doesn't count!

Brian grins. Both boys are excited. Someone in a Darth Vader costume walks by. He's followed by a Luke and a Leia in full costume.

> JEFF (CONT'D)
> Sure you don't want to join us, Dad?

> PAPA (O.S.)
> Nah, I'm meeting a buddy at the bar across the way.

There's a game on. I'll be back at 9:15 p.m. to pick
you up.

                    JEFF
Okay. See you later!

They wave at the camera.

                _____

EXT. UPTOWN THEATER—LATER
Again, on the street outside the theater. People are streaming out
of the 7:00 p.m. screening.

                    PAPA (O.S.)
And now we are waiting for Jeff and Brian to appear,
pumped up after watching the destruction of the
Death Star!

He begins to hum the *Star Wars* theme to himself. He catches
a glimpse of Jeff and Brian in the line of people. But Jeff walks
quickly, staring at the floor, and Brian has to struggle to keep up
with him.

                    BRIAN
It's okay. I don't care. You know my uncle—

                    JEFF
I don't want to talk about it.

                    PAPA (O.S.)
Talk about what?

Jeff looks up, surprised, almost as if he had forgotten his father was going to be there.

>   JEFF
>   Nothing. Let's go home.

>   PAPA (O.S.)
>   I thought we were going to go get ice cream?

>   BRIAN
>   It's okay, Mr. Dalton. Jeff isn't feeling well.

Jeff stares at the sidewalk, avoiding everyone's gaze.

>   PAPA (O.S.)
>   Is everything okay?

>   JEFF
>   It's fine. I just have a headache. Where's the car?

The screen goes black.

I WAS CONFUSED WHEN the tape ended. Was *this* the movie my father had wanted me to watch? If so, why? It was just him and a friend at the movies. It didn't mean a thing to me at the time, except "*Star Wars* puzzle." But later . . .

You'll see.

Walter Dalton's Cell Phone | Wednesday, July 8, 2015, 10:45 p.m.

VOICE MEMO

[RECORDING BEGINS]

I don't know about this, Lily. Claudia is convinced she's going to see her dad again tomorrow. And . . . I don't know. Something seems off. Why make this so complicated? Why not just tell us what's going on?

But you should have seen how excited Claudia was. Her eyes shining, her ponytail bobbing up and down as she ran around the room, leaving her mother the most incoherent voice mail message I've ever heard. I don't know what Jenny will think. We missed her call today, and she's asleep now because of the time difference.

Claudia also found an old videotape in the puzzle box. It was a home movie of me taking Jeff and a friend to the movies. I didn't even remember it, but watching the video made me a little sad. Why didn't I go to the movies with Jeff? Sure, I'm not a science fiction fan—give me a good documentary, please—but really. It wouldn't have hurt me to watch *Star Wars* one more time.

Anyway, I said I'd take Claudia and her little friend to the museum tomorrow, so I'd better get some sleep. We'll see what happens . . .

[RECORDING ENDS]

YOUR TRIP TO:

Smithsonian National Air and Space Museum

20 minutes   8.8 miles

Driving time based on traffic as of 5:15 PM on July 9, 2015.

Current Traffic: Heavy

- Turn right onto W Masonic View Ave
- Turn left onto Russell Rd
- Turn left onto W Braddock Rd
- Turn right onto Valley Dr
- Turn left onto Dogwood Dr
- Turn right onto N Quaker Ln
- Merge onto I-395 N toward Washington
- Use the two left lanes to take US-1 N exit toward Downtown
- Continue onto US-1 N/14th St SW
- Turn right onto Independence Ave SW
  Your destination will be on the left.

Smithsonian National Air and Space Museum

600 Independence Ave SW

Washington, DC

Museum Store
Smithsonian Air and Space Museum
601 Independence Ave SW
Washington, DC 20001

Order #: 68261   Date: 07/09/2015
                                  Time: 8:35 PM

_____

1 Astronaut Ice Cream (chocolate)   3.99
1 Astronaut Ice Cream (vanilla)   3.99
1 Astronaut Ice Cream (strawberry)   3.99
Subtotal: 11.97

Tax: 1.20
Total: 13.17

_____

Thank You For Shopping With Us!

From: Claudia Dalton <claudiadalton195@gmail.com>
Date: Thursday, July 9, 2015 10:15 PM EST
To: Jeffery Dalton <jeffdalton327@gmail.com>
Subject: Skylab

Dear Dad,

I waited. I waited for you for THREE HOURS at the entrance to Skylab. But you didn't show up! From 5:45 p.m. until the museum closed at 9:00 p.m. Why would you do that? Why would you send me that flyer and the puzzle piece and tell me to watch those videos if you didn't want me to come? If you didn't want to see me?

Luis waited with me the whole time, clutching his video camera. He thought he was going to get a shot of us reuniting, you know, like they show on the news. Instead, I spent the entire time walking in and out of that stupid space station, looking at the packets of freeze-dried food, the sleeping bags Velcroed to the wall, and the huge tube-shaped shower, until I had memorized every square inch.

Papa came to get us when it was time to go. He had bought some astronaut ice cream and wanted to sit on the front steps of the museum and eat it before we drove home. We sat by a statue out front, a big stainless steel arrow with spiky stars at the top.

I knew Papa was trying to make me feel better, but the ice cream was disgusting. I always think it's going to taste good—I mean, it's freeze-dried ice cream!—but then it's always so gross and powdery. It gets my hopes up and then disappoints me. Kinda like you.
Love, Claudia

[RECORDING BEGINS]

Oh, Lily, of course he didn't show. I'm so sad for Claudia. She was so disappointed. Wish I could do more for her than buy ice cream!

Which was awful, by the way. I always think that freeze-dried stuff is going to taste good, and it never does.

[RECORDING ENDS]

Claudia Dalton's Cell Phone | Thursday, July 9, 2015, 10:25 p.m.

KATE

How'd it go at the museum?
Did he show up?

No

I'm so sorry

Sigh

Wanna talk?

Not really

Okay
Call you tomorrow

AFTER I EMAILED Dad, I went up into the attic, sat on the old couch, and stared at the shelf of puzzles. I pulled the Skylab piece and the folded list of all 105 puzzles out of my pocket. I pretty much always had them with me. The piece and the list felt like a link to my father.

But what was I doing? Why was I still sending him emails if he wasn't going to answer? Maybe it was pointless. Maybe I should give up.

I twirled the puzzle piece between my fingers, looking at the black background with the white dots. What could it be? Which puzzle did it belong to? I had been so excited when we figured out the *Star Wars* puzzle. I wanted to have that feeling again.

Skylab.

Star Wars.

Stars . . .

And that's when I realized what it was.

Claudia Dalton's Cell Phone | Thursday, July 9, 2015, 10:37 p.m.

Luis: Hello?

Claudia: They're stars!

Luis: Huh?

Claudia: The white dots on the black puzzle piece. They are stars!

Luis: What?

Claudia: There's a puzzle called "Orbiting Earth." It shows Skylab with the Earth in the background, surrounded by empty space and stars.

Luis: So the flyer telling you to go to the museum wasn't because your dad was going to be there—

Claudia: He was giving us a clue to the next puzzle!

Luis: Your dad is cool.

Claudia: My dad is an idiot. But you'll come over tomorrow, right?

Luis: Of course.

Claudia: It's a thousand pieces. So maybe you could actually help work the puzzle this time and not just film me doing it?

Luis: [LAUGHING] I'll bring my tripod.

Claudia: Thanks, Luis.

Luis: Sure thing.

INT. PAPA'S KITCHEN—DAY

Luis and Claudia sit at the kitchen island. Claudia opens the "Orbiting Earth" puzzle. The pieces are tiny, about half the size of the *Star Wars* pieces. There's also another videotape. Luis picks it up.

                    LUIS
          What's this? The label says "Skylab."

                    CLAUDIA
          I don't know. There was an old home movie in the *Star
          Wars* puzzle too. Maybe this is another one?

                    LUIS
          Want to watch it now?

Claudia shakes her head.

                    CLAUDIA
          We should probably wait for Papa.

Luis shrugs and hands it to her. Claudia puts the tape aside and turns back to the puzzle. For a few minutes, they sort the pieces without speaking, as music plays softly on Claudia's phone.

                    LUIS
          You okay?

                    CLAUDIA
          Yeah.

She stares intently at her pieces.

CLAUDIA (CONT'D)

I appreciate you helping me.

LUIS

No problem.

Claudia glances up at Luis. He's examining a corner piece. He glances at her. She quickly looks back at her pieces.

CLAUDIA

And I wanted to say I was sorry for yelling at you at the movies the other day.

LUIS

It's okay.

CLAUDIA

No, it was rude.

LUIS

I spilled my soda on you! And I was already embarrassed because I forgot to bring money for popcorn.

CLAUDIA

You were embarrassed?

LUIS

Yeah.

CLAUDIA

It's okay. I'm sorry we had to leave the movie.

                              LUIS

I don't really like zombie movies anyway.

                            CLAUDIA

What?!

                              LUIS

I wanted to see *Inside Out* but thought you'd think I
was weird.

                            CLAUDIA

I would have thought you were weird. But I wanted to
see *Inside Out* too!

                              LUIS

Really?

                            CLAUDIA

Yeah.

                              LUIS

Oh.

                            CLAUDIA

Why didn't you wait for me so we could pick the movie
together?

                              LUIS

It was a rainy day! I was afraid the movie would sell
out.

Claudia laughs.

LUIS (CONT'D)

What's so funny?

CLAUDIA

I worry about stuff like that too.

LUIS

Or we'd have to sit in the front row. I *hate* sitting in the front row. Always get a crick in my neck.

CLAUDIA

I know!

They do a few more pieces in silence.

LUIS

I should say sorry too. It probably wasn't the nicest to insist you tell your story so I could film it.

CLAUDIA

Well . . .

LUIS

My teacher is always telling me, in a documentary, you can't treat people like they're actors. You gotta make sure they know you really care about them.

CLAUDIA

Is that why you're helping me? For the story?

LUIS

No.

                    CLAUDIA
    Then why?

Luis shrugs.

                    LUIS
    I like puzzles.

Claudia smiles and looks over at the camera. Luis notices.

                    LUIS (CONT'D)
    Don't worry, no one ever wants to watch my videos
    anyway. I can't even get my mom to . . . I'll turn it off
    if you want.

                    CLAUDIA
    No, it's okay.

They work a few more puzzle pieces.

                    CLAUDIA (CONT'D)
    You think my story is interesting?

                    LUIS
    Absolutely.

                    CLAUDIA
    So, what do you want to know?

                    LUIS
    Really? You don't mind?

Claudia shrugs.

                    CLAUDIA
     Go ahead. Ask away.

                    LUIS
     Were your parents having problems?

Claudia stares at her pieces for a long moment, putting a few in
place.

                    CLAUDIA
     I don't think so.

                    LUIS
     You're lucky, then. I knew my parents were going to
     get divorced before they did.

                    CLAUDIA
     What do you mean?

                    LUIS
     They fought all the time! I mean all the time. Dad was
     always starting a new business, always dreaming up
     a new scheme. For literally ten years. And nothing
     worked.

                    CLAUDIA
     And your mom supported him all that time?

                    LUIS
     Yup. She's a lawyer. Earns plenty of money, but Dad

kept coming up with a new idea and burning through their savings. Finally, Mom had enough and divorced him.

                    CLAUDIA

I'm sorry.

                    LUIS

No, it's better. Dad gave up working for himself and got a programming job. I think he kinda likes it. He's super smart, but not so good at being his own boss. And Mom, well, she married Stewart and had my little sister, Mariana. I miss seeing her during the year, but . . . it's okay.

                    CLAUDIA

Oh.

She works some more puzzle pieces.

                    LUIS

I'm not saying that's going to happen to your parents.

                    CLAUDIA

Good. Because that's not going to happen to my parents.

                    LUIS

Just, if it did, you'd be okay.

Claudia glares at him, then turns her attention back to the puzzle.

                    LUIS (CONT'D)
Did I say the wrong thing again?

                    CLAUDIA
Yes.

Luis laughs. Claudia smiles a little too. They both keep working on
the puzzle.

From: Claudia Dalton <claudiadalton195@gmail.com>
Date: Friday, July 10, 2015 1:03 PM EST
To: Jeffery Dalton <jeffdalton327@gmail.com>
Subject: Orbiting Earth

Dear Dad,

I'm sorry I was grumpy last night. I guess I misunderstood your clues. It's some sort of a treasure hunt, right? Like the one you did on Easter when I was little, where one clue led to another. But this time, the prize at the end is finding you. Right?

Anyway, Luis came over right after breakfast and we started on "Orbiting Earth." The funny thing about working a puzzle is it kind of makes it easier to talk. You don't have to look at the person; you have something to do with your hands. Maybe that's why when Luis asked if you and Mom had been having problems, I didn't tell him to shut up.

Instead, I thought about Kate's parents. Sure, they work a lot, but whenever I see them, they're really sweet to each other. Sometimes they hold hands during dinner. And when her mom walks by her dad in the hallway, he always swats her on the butt and she giggles like a teenager. Kate and I roll our eyes and say, "Ewww, gross," but inside I sometimes think about how you and Mom never play around like that, and it makes me a little sad.

But you and Mom don't fight much, so after about three or four pieces, I said no. Is that the truth? Luis's parents are divorced, but it's not going to be like that for us. Right? I mean, we'll work it all out when you come home, won't we? You always say you can work anything out with enough time and patience.

Anyway, I better go. Papa and I are going to watch the "Skylab" video over lunch. And then Luis is going to come back over for more puzzles.

Love, Claudia

EXT. AIR AND SPACE MUSEUM

The camera focuses on a statue in front of the Air and Space Museum. It's a long metal point with spiky stars at the top. The camera pans down the statue to reveal a huge group of schoolkids standing in a group.

TEACHER

Please find your chaperones and stay together.

DWIGHT

We're in seventh grade. Don't know why we still need chaperones.

JEFF

Dad! Over here.

Papa wanders over.

PAPA (O.S.)

Who else is in our group?

Brian walks up to them. He's wearing a striped shirt.

BRIAN

Are you Mr. Dalton?

PAPA (O.S.)

Yes.

BRIAN

I think I'm in your group, sir. New camcorder?

PAPA (O.S.)

Yup. Got it last month for my birthday.

BRIAN

Nice.

PAPA (O.S.)

It records on VHS tapes you put right in your VCR. No
cables needed.

BRIAN

Pretty cool.

———

INT. SKYLAB—DAY

The group of boys and Papa walk through the Skylab exhibit.
Dwight and Jason laugh at the "space shower," a big plastic tube
where the astronauts could bathe.

DWIGHT

You ain't never gonna find me showering in a tube.
Everyone looking at my stuff.

BRIAN

That why you smell? Never shower after gym class,
huh?

DWIGHT

Shut up, new kid.

BRIAN

Wow, that was clever. Really clever.

Dwight turns to Jason.

                    DWIGHT
        Come on, let's go look at something else.

Dwight and Jason walk off-camera.

                    JEFF
        Quick on your feet.

                    BRIAN
        Gotta be. We move a lot. Dad's military.

                    JEFF
        Oh.

                    BRIAN
        I'm Brian.

                    JEFF
        Jeff. You already met my dad.

                    PAPA (O.S.)
        Hello!

                    JEFF
        Dad, put the camera away. I don't want you to miss
        anything.

Walter Dalton's Cell Phone | Friday, July 10, 2015, 1:47 p.m.

[RECORDING BEGINS]

Lily, I had forgotten about chaperoning that trip. You were supposed to go, but you had the flu, and you didn't want to cancel and leave the teacher in a bind. So you made me take the day off work and go instead. I was so mad about it!

And yet, Jeff actually wanted me there. Why didn't I see that then?

[RECORDING ENDS]

Claudia Dalton's Cell Phone | Friday, July 10, 2015, 3:45 p.m.

PHONE TRANSCRIPT

Claudia: Hi, Mom.

Mom: Oh, Claudia. Papa texted me. You must have been so disappointed when your father didn't show at the museum.

Claudia: I don't want to talk about it.

Mom: Okay. [PAUSE] So, what are you doing today?

Claudia: Luis and I are working a puzzle.

Mom: Luis?

Claudia: The neighbor kid.

Mom: Oh, he's helping you with the puzzles?! Nice. I'm glad you're making friends.

Claudia: We also found these old videotapes from when Dad was a kid.

Mom: Really? Do you think those were the ones he wanted you to watch?

Claudia: Maybe. Mom, can I ask you something?

Mom: Of course!

Claudia: It's kinda weird. And embarrassing. Not something we usually talk about. But Luis was asking me all these questions, and I figured maybe I could ask you too.

Mom: Claudia, you can ask me anything.

Claudia: Okay. Well then . . . were you and Dad having problems? Marriage problems, I mean.

Mom: Oh.

Claudia: You don't have to answer if you don't want to. It's just, Luis's parents are divorced and we were talking about it and . . .

Mom: No, it's fine, Claudia. With your father gone, of course you would wonder. [PAUSE] Yeah, I think we were.

Claudia: You were?

Mom: I mean, if you had asked me a month ago, I would have said no. But now . . .

Claudia: But you and Dad hardly ever argue.

Mom: I'm not sure that's a good thing. I think your father checked out a while ago, and I didn't even notice.

Claudia: Were you having money problems?

Mom: No, no money problems.

Claudia: Because Luis's dad was really bad with money and that's why they split up.

Mom: No one is splitting up, Claudia. Not yet.

Claudia: But you might, right?

Mom: [SILENCE]

Claudia: Mom?

Mom: It is a possibility.

Claudia: I don't want you to split up.

Mom: Your father abandoned us, Claudia. With no explanation.

Claudia: He said he needed time to think things over.

Mom: But what things? I'm racking my brain and I can't think of anything.

Claudia: Maybe I did something—

Mom: No! Claudia, it was definitely not you. Your father loves you. He's sending you these clues, right?

Claudia: Yeah. I know you think they're stupid, but—

Mom: I don't think they're stupid. I think there's something he wants to tell you.

Claudia: What?

Mom: I wish I knew, Claudia.

Claudia: I gotta go. Luis is back with more chips and soda.

Mom: Good luck with the puzzle.

Claudia: Thanks. Is your conference going okay?

Mom: Yes, it's fine. Even had a little time to sit by the pool and think.

Claudia: Good.

Mom: Thanks for asking, sweetie. I love you.

Claudia: Love you too.

INT. PAPA'S KITCHEN—DAY

Luis is filming again. The "Orbiting Earth" puzzle is almost complete. Claudia puts a red-and-white-striped piece into the flag painted on the side of the space station. She presses two black pieces with stars into place.

                    CLAUDIA
        Do you have the "Skylab" piece?

Luis hands it to her. She presses it into place. It fits perfectly.

                    LUIS (O.S.)
        There's one piece left over.

The piece is blue. A regular piece. Two tabs, two pockets.

                    LUIS (O.S.) (CONT'D)
        Is there a message on the back?

Claudia turns it over. Luis zooms in.

"Horns on Uncle Beazley" is handwritten in pencil. The letter *I* is written on one corner.

                    CLAUDIA
        Yes.

                    LUIS
        It's kind of cool how one piece leads to another. It's a
        treasure hunt.

Claudia doesn't say a word.

Horns on Uncle
Beazley

I

From: Claudia Dalton <claudiadalton195@gmail.com>

Date: Friday, July 10, 2015 8:08 PM EST

To: Jeffery Dalton <jeffdalton327@gmail.com>

Subject: Who is Uncle Beazley?

Dear Dad,

We finished the puzzle. We found the next piece.

But all I could think was: Why are you doing this? Who is Uncle Beazley? Why does he have horns? What do the letters mean? Why do you want me to watch your old home movies? Why can't you just come home?

Love, Claudia

Claudia Dalton's Cell Phone | Saturday, July 11, 2015, 10:30 a.m.

TEXT MESSAGE

KATE

I googled Uncle Beazley
He's a fiberglass statue of a dinosaur!
Donated to the Natural History Museum
Been at the zoo since 1994

Is there a puzzle of a dinosaur?

There are a bunch of dinosaur puzzles!
Stegosaurus and Friends
T-Rex on the Loose
Pterodactyls Attack
We're going to visit the statue to
see if it helps us narrow things down

Cool
What does the "I" mean?
Or the "R" on the other piece?

No clue
What are you doing today?

Mom's friends are throwing
her a baby shower tonight

Yummy
Cake!

I'm not going

Why not?
Weren't you invited?

Course I was invited
Mom's begging me to go

But . . .

But what?

But I'm not excited about the baby
I don't want to have to go and fake it

Oh

What?

Well, you were right about Luis

What do you mean?

I'm glad you convinced me to give him
another chance after the movie incident
He's really nice

So you think I should go?

All I'm saying is, if you have to
have a brother, maybe you
should try to be a little excited
At least go and eat free cake!

Haha. I'll think about it.

SMITHSONIAN NATIONAL ZOOLOGICAL PARK

————————————————————

PARKING RECEIPT

————————————————————

TYPE: CAR PARKING
DATE: 7/11/15
TIME: 11:05 AM

PAID: $25.00
VISA:
XXXX-XXXX-XXXX-5921

————————————————————

THANK YOU AND DRIVE SAFELY!

————————————————————

EXT. ZOO—DAY

Blue sky. Some trees. An elephant wanders by.

       LUIS

  No, you push that button there.

       CLAUDIA (O.S.)

  This one?

The camera zooms in on Luis's face.

       LUIS

  Yeah.

       CLAUDIA (O.S.)

  Wave.

Luis waves at the camera.

————

EXT. ZOO—LATER

Papa and Luis walk side by side while Claudia films them.

       LUIS

  So, my mom was really mad when my dad bought me
  the camera.

       PAPA

  Mad? Why?

Luis shrugs.

LUIS

My mom came here as a baby. They didn't have a lot
of money growing up. So she does *not* like the idea of
me doing anything artistic. Doctor, lawyer, engineer.
That's what I'm supposed to be.

They stop by a small waterfall.

LUIS (CONT'D)

I don't get it. The map says it's right . . .

PAPA

There! There it is.

He points. Sure enough, behind a low metal fence, hidden in a
bunch of tall bushes, is a huge fiberglass triceratops.

It's surprisingly lifelike. About nine feet tall, and over twenty
feet long. His three horns point straight at the camera, the two
big ones by his eyes, and the small one on his snout too. His skin is
mottled and his bony frill protects his neck. There is a sign in front
of the statue that says KEEP OFF THE DINOSAUR.

CLAUDIA (O.S.)

It feels like it's looking at us.

Papa's face twitches. He blinks a few times and scratches an eye-
brow. Finally, he covers his face with his hands and his shoulders
start to shake.

CLAUDIA (O.S.)

Papa. Are you okay?

                              PAPA

          I'm fine.

But he doesn't take his hands away from his face.

                          CLAUDIA (O.S.)

          You're crying.

Papa wipes his eyes.

                              PAPA

          I'm not crying! I just need to sit down.

He turns and sits on a nearby bench. Sweat beads on Papa's forehead. Luis pulls a bottle of water out of his backpack and hands it
to Papa. He takes a long, long sip.

                          PAPA (CONT'D)

          Thank you. I feel better now.

                          CLAUDIA (O.S.)

          What . . . what happened?

                              PAPA

          When he was little, Jeff used to play on this
          dinosaur in front of the Natural History Museum.
          He loved dinosaurs. I didn't approve. I thought it was
          silly.

He glances at Luis.

PAPA (CONT'D)

I guess I had pretty firm ideas about what he was
supposed to be too.

Claudia hands the camera to Luis. He refocuses quickly. Claudia
sits down next to her grandfather on the bench and puts her head
on his shoulder. They sit like that for a long time.

Walter Dalton's Cell Phone | Saturday, July 11, 2015, 1:15 p.m.

[RECORDING BEGINS]

Lily, this therapy is not helping. It's making everything worse! I've never broken down like this. I started crying at the zoo. It was so embarrassing. I gave the kids twenty bucks and told them to go buy themselves some ice cream. Now I'm sitting in the car, talking to my phone, trying to pull myself together.

'Cause we can't just go home. Oh, no. Claudia wants to go to the Natural History Museum, since that's where the Uncle Beazley dinosaur used to be. *Still too many possible puzzles. We have to narrow it down.*

I can't tell her no. Because . . . because maybe if I had been more involved . . .

Maybe if I had been more involved, more understanding, less judgmental, a better father, maybe Jeff would not have left. Maybe he would have just told us what was going on. Maybe this is all my fault.

[RECORDING ENDS]

Smithsonian National Museum
of Natural History
10th St. & Constitution Ave. NW
Washington, DC 20560

Saturday, July 11, 2015
2:31 PM

MAMMAL STORE
First Floor
Kenneth E. Behring Family Hall of Mammals
10:00 AM—5:30 PM

1 plush animal	
(Baby Triceratops)	9.99
1 "Dinos Rule" onesie	
size 0-3 months	12.00
Subtotal:	21.99
Tax:	1.26
Total:	23.25

INT. NATURAL HISTORY MUSEUM—DAY

Claudia stands in the rotunda. She points at a huge stuffed elephant.

> CLAUDIA
>
> Apparently, his name is Henry.

> PAPA
>
> This thing has been here since Jeff was a kid.

> LUIS (O.S.)
>
> Any elephant puzzles?

Claudia pulls the list of puzzles out of her pocket.

> CLAUDIA
>
> "Elephants of the Wild." Five hundred pieces.

Papa walks over to a security guard.

> PAPA
>
> Where are the dinosaurs?

> GUARD
>
> Fossil Hall is closed until 2019.

Papa looks like he's about to cry again. Claudia rushes over and takes his arm.

> CLAUDIA
>
> It's okay. We'll just look at other stuff.

———

INT. NATURAL HISTORY MUSEUM—LATER
Ocean exhibit. A huge life-size model of a blue whale hangs from the ceiling.

                         PAPA
     Is there a whale puzzle?

                         CLAUDIA
     Maybe "The Giant of the Deep"? Two hundred fifty
     pieces.

                    ———————

INT. NATURAL HISTORY MUSEUM—LATER
Close-up of a sparkly necklace with a huge blue jewel. It's displayed in a thick glass case, and the pedestal it's on rotates slowly.

                         PAPA
     The Hope Diamond.

                         CLAUDIA (O.S.)
     Could it be "Rocks and Gems"? That's only a hundred
     pieces.

                         LUIS
     I hope it's that one.

                         CLAUDIA (O.S.)
     Haha.

                         PAPA
     It's also called "The Cursed Jewel."

CLAUDIA (O.S.)

Ooh, that's on the list too. Two hundred pieces.

———

INT. NATURAL HISTORY MUSEUM—LATER

Claudia stands in front of a huge crystal ball, staring into the glass.

PAPA

Come on, Claudia. It's time to go.

WHEN WE GOT home, we had seven puzzle possibilities. Luis and I found the puzzles on the shelf and looked at the pieces before we started working them. The cardboard on the back of the Uncle Beazley piece was blue. The cardboard on the back of "Stegosaurus," "Elephants," and "Giant" was brown. "T-Rex," "The Cursed Jewel" and "Rocks & Gems" were gray. And "Pterodactyls" was a weird beige color. So none of those were right.

Luis started pulling the boxes off the shelves and looking at the pictures on top. Sometimes you can't tell from the title what it is. Like how the "Orbiting Earth" puzzle didn't mention Skylab. So we decided just to look. We were about halfway through when we found one called "The Gentle Giant."

It was a scene from a museum, with a crowd of people gathered around a triceratops. When we opened the box, the cardboard on the back of the pieces was blue. And there was a VHS tape labled "Uncle Beazley."

INT. NATURAL HISTORY MUSEUM—DAY

A group of kids and parents wait in the rotunda, a huge stuffed elephant looming over their heads. Jeff stands with his ear to a white wand with a cord attached to the exhibit. A boy comes over and taps him on the shoulder.

                    BRIAN
          Hey! What are you doing here?

                    JEFF
          I'm signed up for the Dinolab class.

                    BRIAN
          The one where you get the behind-the-scenes tour of
          where they excavate the bones?

                    JEFF
          Yeah.

                    BRIAN
          Me too!

He grins.

                    BRIAN (CONT'D)
          If they put us into groups, we should team up.

                    JEFF
          Yeah. Yeah, that sounds good.

Jeff smiles.

                              WOMAN
         Dinolab! Over here, please.

A group of twelve-year-old boys shuffles toward her.

                         ————————

EXT. NATURAL HISTORY MUSEUM—DAY
There's a big plastic model of a triceratops on the mall in front of
the museum. Brian and Jeff climb up the front, hanging off the
horns. Two women stand nearby, watching the boys.

                         BRIAN'S MOM
         Your son is Jeff, right?

                              NANA
         Yes.

                         BRIAN'S MOM
         I'm Lucile. Brian's mom.

                              NANA
         I'm Lily. Nice to meet you.

                         BRIAN'S MOM
         Jeff seems like a really nice boy.

                              NANA
         He is.

                         PAPA (O.S.)
         But who ever heard of a kid wanting to study science
         on the weekend instead of signing up for soccer?

Brian's mom laughs.

                    BRIAN'S MOM
        It's not that odd. Brian likes science and soccer.

The boys climb over the dinosaur's frill, sit on the top of its back
for a moment, and slide down its tail. Lily turns to the camera.

                    NANA
        Walter, watch my purse.

Without waiting for an answer, Lily strides over to the dinosaur.
She puts her hands on her hips and studies it for a moment before
grabbing the horns, putting her foot on the nose, and pulling herself up.
        The boys cheer.

Walter Dalton's Cell Phone | Saturday, July 11, 2015, 7:30 p.m.

[RECORDING BEGINS]

Apparently, this is the day for embarrassing myself. I certainly didn't expect to get all teary-eyed watching some old home movie.

But I did. When you marched over and climbed up onto that dinosaur, I laughed out loud. You looked so pretty and young. I wished I had told you how much I loved it when you did silly things like that. I wish I had been more like you.

Well, with Claudia, maybe now I have a second chance. Don't want to waste it.

[RECORDING ENDS]

From: Claudia Dalton <claudiadalton195@gmail.com>
Date: Saturday, July 11, 2015 9:09 PM EST
To: Jeffery Dalton <jeffdalton327@gmail.com>
Subject: Uncle Beazley

Dear Dad,

Uncle Beazley!! We found a video of you and Nana on Uncle Beazley. That was so cool! When did you write these clues? A bunch of them are out-of-date. Seems like it might have been a long time ago.

But it's funny, 'cause they all remind me of stuff I've done with you. Like that time when you played with me on the monkey bars. We both hung upside down and you were so tall, your hands reached the ground. You looked just like you did on Uncle Beazley. Is that why you wanted me to watch them?

Anyway, we found the next puzzle, "The Gentle Giant," and finished it tonight. It was only 300 pieces. And sure enough, there was one piece left over, red on the front, beige cardboard on the back, with a clue written in pencil.

Love, Claudia

PS. Did you ever look into the crystal ball in the gems and jewels exhibit at the Natural History Museum? I spent a long time there today, trying to see when you would come home.

Bobs on the pendulum B

Claudia Dalton's Cell Phone | Sunday, July 12, 2015, 9:15 a.m.

KATE

> Okay, I'll say it
> You were right
> The baby shower last night was actually fun

I'm glad

> We played a game where you
> had to change a diaper on a doll
> And I won!
> Learned how to do that in the class

Cool

> Mom got so many presents, she said
> I could have the Target gift card

Nice

> And the cake was yummy too

Good

> Claudia, are you okay?
> Cause you're texting like my dad

Sorry, I'm just eating breakfast
We found another puzzle piece last night

> What?!

It's red on the front
Says "Bobs on the pendulum" on the back

Who the heck is Bob?
And why is he on a pendulum?

Haha
Google pendulum
A bob is the little weight thingie at the end

Is there a puzzle of a pendulum?

No

So what are you going to do?
Work all the puzzles with red?

Too many
But Papa says there's a pendulum
at the American History Museum
We're gonna check it out

Is your boyfriend going too?

Haha

Well, is he?

No, his mom is sick and he
has to babysit his little sister

Oh well. Next time. Have fun with Papa

Thanks

Trip Planner

Trip Planner Results

From KING STREET METRO STATION
To SMITHSONIAN METRO STATION

Leaving at 10:00 AM | Sunday, July 12, 2015

ITINERARY 1—24 MINS
Leave at: 10:10 am
Arrive at 10:33 am

YL KING STREET METRO STATION
Yellow Line to FORT TOTTEN
Exit at L'ENFANT PLAZA METRO STATION

OR L'ENFANT PLAZA METRO STATION
Orange Line to VIENNA FAIRFAX–GMU
Exit at SMITHSONIAN METRO STATION

$2.75 SmarTrip Fare
$1.70 SmarTrip (Senior/Disabled/Medicare)

STARS AND STRIPES CAFÉ
National Museum of American History
14th Street and Constitution Avenue, NW
Washington, DC 20001

Order #: 68261   Date: 7/12/15
Server: Cashier 2   Time: 12:53 PM

———————————————————————

1 Diet Coke	2.99
1 Dr Pepper	2.99
1 Cherry Pie	3.00
1 Chocolate Pudding	2.99
1 Ice Cream Sundae	3.50
1 Coffee	3.00
Subtotal:	18.47
Tax:	1.85
Total:	20.32

———————————————————————

Thank You For Dining With Us!

INT. AMERICAN HISTORY MUSEUM—DAY

Papa walks through the front doors. There's a metal flag on the wall in front of them, but no pendulum. Papa looks around, bewildered.

> PAPA
>
> I don't understand. I could have sworn it was right here!

———

INT. AMERICAN HISTORY MUSEUM—LATER

Papa talks to a museum guard while Claudia films them. The guard is so old, even his beard is white.

> GUARD
>
> Yup. There was a pendulum. My kids and I used to love to come and watch it. Everyone would cheer when the bob would knock one of the pegs down.

> PAPA
>
> So what happened to it?

> GUARD
>
> Well, it was a Foucault pendulum, you see. Named after the French physicist Jean Foucault. He invented it in 1851 to demonstrate the rotation of the Earth. Some bigwig museum planner got it in his head that there shouldn't be an invention from a French physicist in the lobby of a museum about American history.

He shrugs.

> GUARD (CONT'D)
>
> So they removed it. Packed up the whole thing and
> put it in storage.

He shakes his head.

> GUARD (CONT'D)
>
> Progress. Y'all enjoy the rest of your visit.

___

INT. AMERICAN HISTORY MUSEUM—LATER

Papa walks through the "Star-Spangled Banner" exhibit.

> CLAUDIA (O.S.)
>
> It's so dark!

> PAPA
>
> The flag used to be in the lobby. Could see it a lot
> better then.

> GUARD 2
>
> Miss, there's no photography allowed in here. The
> flag's very delicate.

> CLAUDIA (O.S.)
>
> Sorry!

___

INT. AMERICAN HISTORY MUSEUM—LATER

First ladies' gowns exhibit: Claudia stares at Michelle Obama's
Jimmy Choo shoes from the first inauguration.

How did she walk in those?

Claudia laughs.

INT. AMERICAN HISTORY MUSEUM—LATER

Claudia looks at a huge old dollhouse, with five floors and twenty-three rooms. Papa walks up to her and puts a hand on her shoulder.

She turns and smiles at him.

From: Claudia Dalton <claudiadalton195@gmail.com>
Date: Sunday, July 12, 2015 4:09 PM EST
To: Jeffery Dalton <jeffdalton327@gmail.com>
Subject: The Dollhouse and the Pendulum

Dear Dad,

Papa and I went to the American History Museum today. The pendulum isn't there anymore, but we saw the flag, and the first ladies' gowns, and the dollhouse.

I guess that must be the next puzzle, because there is one called "The Dollhouse." But I don't see what that has to do with a pendulum. Still, the pieces are the right size, and the cardboard on the back is beige, just like on the red piece with *Bobs on the Pendulum*. But there was no VHS tape in the box. Maybe you just didn't put one in this time? But if we're doing the wrong puzzle, please send another clue!

Love, Claudia

Luis: Hello?

Claudia: Hi, it's me. How's your mom?

Luis: She's much better, thanks. How was the museum?

Claudia: Good. I think I found the next puzzle. And spending the day alone with Papa wasn't as awkward as I expected. We actually had fun!

Luis: I'm so glad. I was a little worried about him. I mean, he got so upset at the zoo and . . .

Claudia: I'm sorry it was weird.

Luis: No, no. I know how he feels. When Mom first left, sometimes everything seemed normal. Like she was just at work or something. And then other times . . . it would hit me. All at once.

Claudia: Yeah. Yeah, that happens to me too.

Luis: You can call me if it does. I mean, if you feel upset like your grandpa, you can call me.

Claudia: Thanks. But it's usually late at night. Wouldn't want to bother you.

Luis: Not a bother. That's what friends do.

Claudia: Are we friends?

Luis: Aren't we?

Claudia: Yeah. I think we are.

Luis: Good.

Claudia: Soo . . . "The Dollhouse" puzzle tomorrow?

Luis: Wouldn't miss it.

[RECORDING BEGINS]

Okay, Lily, I admit it. Maybe there's something to that doctor and trying new things.

Because Claudia and I had fun today. We took the Metro into the city instead of driving. We had dessert for lunch. And she asked me to help film at the museum. We only had her phone instead of Luis's good camera, but it worked.

And I remembered why I liked it. Behind the camera, I could be part of the action without saying anything. I felt safe. I wish I had done more with Jeff, but I was there. I showed up!

I'm glad Claudia and I are watching all those old videos. I feel like something is waking up inside me and . . .

Something waking up inside me? Me talking about touchy-feely crap? An alien, it must be an alien waking up inside me, like in a horror movie.

Kidding, Lily. I know you hate horror movies. I just miss you.

[RECORDING ENDS]

L UIS CAME OVER the next morning and we were busy working the "Dollhouse" puzzle, listening to music on my phone, when the most embarrassing thing happened . . .

Claudia Dalton's Cell Phone | Monday, July 13, 2015, 9:30 a.m.

Summer Songs Playlist

[▶ PLAY]   [⤨ SHUFFLE]

1. Cheerleader (Felix Jaehn Remix)
   OMI

2. Marvin Gaye
   Charlie Puth (feat. Meghan Trainor)

3. Uptown Funk
   Mark Ronson (feat. Bruno Mars)

4. Sugar
   Maroon 5

5. Shut Up and Dance
   Walk the Moon

6. Fight Song
   Rachel Platten

7. The Star-Spangled Banner
   Whitney Houston

8. Honey, I'm Good.
   Andy Grammer

9. Heartbeat Song
   Kelly Clarkson

10. Bad Blood
    Taylor Swift

11. Cool for the Summer
    Demi Lovato

Mom: Hello?

Claudia: Mom, did you add "The Star-Spangled Banner" to my Summer Songs Playlist?

Mom: What?

Claudia: Someone added "The Star-Spangled Banner" to my Summer Songs Playlist!

Mom: Claudia, I'm in a meeting. Are you okay?

Claudia: It was super embarrassing! Luis and I were working the "Dollhouse" puzzle and listening to some music when suddenly Whitney Houston started belting out "The Star-Spangled Banner"!

Mom: I don't know what you're talking about.

Claudia: It was a really mean joke!

Mom: Claudia, I didn't do it!

Claudia: Mom, we're on the family plan. Remember? You said you'd pay for it, but only if I made all my playlists collaborative so you could hear everything I was listening to and delete anything you didn't like. The only people who have access to it are you and—

Mom: Claudia, it wasn't me.

Claudia: Oh my gosh, I have to go.

OF COURSE, IT was completely obvious when I looked at the red piece again. There, in one corner, was a silver of white. And sure enough, there was a puzzle on the list called "The Star-Spangled Banner." (How could I have forgotten the video of me singing the national anthem?) When I pulled the puzzle off the shelf, I knew it was the right one, even before I opened the box and found the VHS tape labeled "The Pendulum Project." Because it was actually a picture from the museum, from the old days, when the star-spangled banner was right behind the pendulum.

INT. AMERICAN HISTORY MUSEUM—DAY

Jeff, Brian, and a bunch of other kids lean over the edge of a railing, looking down through a large round hole cut in the floor. A long cable hangs from the ceiling far above them, swinging back and forth in front of a large American flag.

The cable is connected to a pendulum that swings back and forth on the floor below them. There is a circle of pegs on the floor around the pendulum, and every few minutes, the bob knocks over one of the pegs.

The camera zooms in, as the point of the bob hits a peg, causing it to tip. Everyone holds their breath in anticipation. The bob swings back again, hitting the peg more firmly this time and knocking it over. The kids cheer.

Jeff turns to Brian.

JEFF

I have an idea.

INT. STAIRWAY—DAY

A big entryway to a house. There's a staircase with a fancy chandelier at the top. Brian is leaning over the edge of the banister, tightening a loop of fishing line around the light fixture.

JEFF (O.S.)

Careful!

BRIAN

I got it!

Brian drops the line down to the foyer. He runs down the stairs and ties a weight to the end.

                    BRIAN (CONT'D)
This is gonna be the coolest pendulum ever.

                    JEFF (O.S.)
I just hope we get an A on the science fair project.

                    BRIAN
We will! Got the camera ready?

                    JEFF (O.S.)
Yup.

Brian finishes tightening the line, then pulls the weight back and
lets go. Jeff films as the pendulum swings back and forth.

                    BRIAN
Cool! You had a great idea.

                    JEFF (O.S.)
Thanks.

He smiles. The weight swings in a perfect arc.

                    BRIAN
Hmm. We should measure the arc and—

A door opens and Brian's mom enters.

                    BRIAN'S MOM
What are you boys doing to my chandelier?

From: Claudia Dalton <claudiadalton195@gmail.com>

Date: Monday, July 13, 2015 12:30 PM EST

To: Jeffery Dalton <jeffdalton327@gmail.com>

Subject: Whitney Saves the Day

Dear Dad,

Haha, very funny. I got it! Thanks for the clue.

Luis has to babysit his sister this afternoon, so I'm going over to his house to work on the flag and pendulum puzzle now. Oh, and we all liked the video. Hope you didn't break your friend's chandelier!

More soon.

Love, Claudia

INT. LUIS'S DINING ROOM—DAY

Luis's dining room has a huge wooden table with eight chairs. Claudia sits at the head of the table; Luis works beside her. They are sorting pieces, turning them over so they are all picture side up.

                    LUIS

          You know, we could just look for the piece with the
          clue on it.

                    CLAUDIA

          We could. But unless the pendulum piece fits, we can't
          be absolutely sure we have the right puzzle.

                    LUIS

          That's true.

                    CLAUDIA

          And how many clues are there? Does the order we
          find them in matter?

                    LUIS

          I don't know.

                    CLAUDIA

          Neither do I. And also . . .

                    LUIS

          What?

Claudia frowns.

                              CLAUDIA

It's just not as much fun if we look for the piece. Spoils
the game somehow.

Luis thinks for a moment.

                         CLAUDIA (CONT'D)

That sounds stupid, doesn't it?

                               LUIS

No. I think you're right.

                              CLAUDIA

Really?

                               LUIS

Yeah. It's like when my grandma taught me to knit.
We spent all this time and money, and in the end, I
had a lumpy pair of striped socks that cost me forty-
five dollars. But there was something about doing it
myself.

                              CLAUDIA

Yeah. I like that. Wait, you knit?!

                               LUIS

Shut up. I only made the one pair of socks.

Claudia grins. There's a cry from a baby monitor sitting on the
edge of the table.

                          LUIS (CONT'D)

I'll be right back.

He gets up and leaves the room. Claudia works on the puzzle by herself for a few minutes. The camera continues rolling. Finally, Luis returns.

                    LUIS (CONT'D)
Sorry, I had to rock her back to sleep.

He sits down at the table and picks up a couple of pieces.

                    CLAUDIA
How'd you get so good at this?

                    LUIS
At puzzles? Practice.

                    CLAUDIA
No, silly. At taking care of your little sister.

                    LUIS
You gonna tease me about that too?

                    CLAUDIA
No.

                    LUIS
Good. 'Cause I'm not ashamed. I knit AND I change a
mean diaper.

Claudia laughs.

                    CLAUDIA
My best friend back home, her parents are having a
baby. And she's a little freaked out.

                              LUIS

          Tell her it's awful. There's someone newer and
          cuter in the family. No one's going to love her
          anymore!

Claudia stops working the puzzle.

                            CLAUDIA

          Don't say that!

Luis looks confused.

                              LUIS

          I'm just joking.

                            CLAUDIA

          I think she's actually worried.

                              LUIS

          Of course they'll still love her!

                            CLAUDIA

          I know. But . . . her father already doesn't spend a lot
          of time with her. He works really long hours.

                              LUIS

          My mom works really long hours. She loves me.

He sounds a little hurt.

                            CLAUDIA

          I'm sorry, I didn't mean anything by it.

                    LUIS

    It's okay.

They work on the puzzle in silence for a few moments.

                    CLAUDIA

    Why do you live with your dad?

                    LUIS

    Why wouldn't I live with my dad? Only moms can
    take care of kids?

                    CLAUDIA

    Never mind. Everything I'm saying is coming out
    wrong today.

She concentrates on her pieces and blinks rapidly. Luis watches
her, then picks up his own pieces. He doesn't look at her as he talks.

                    LUIS

    I was pretty young when my parents split up. When
    my mom moved out, I was really angry. And I wanted
    to stay at my old school, so the judge gave my father
    primary custody.

                    CLAUDIA

    Oh.

                    LUIS

    I started watching films all the time to fill the hours
    after school. And on the weekends, when the house
    seemed too quiet, my dad and I would go to the movies.

                    CLAUDIA

Nice.

                    LUIS

It was nice! We went almost every weekend. At
home, I wanted to watch something new, but I'd seen
everything. Finally, I discovered documentaries on
Netflix and . . .

He gestures toward the camera.

                    LUIS (CONT'D)

Here I am.

                    CLAUDIA

Are you still angry at your mom?

                    LUIS

No.

                    CLAUDIA

Why not?

Luis shrugs.

                    LUIS

Too hard to explain.

They work the puzzle in silence for a few more minutes.

                    LUIS (CONT'D)

Actually, I do have some advice for your friend.

CLAUDIA

What?

LUIS

She should hold the baby as soon as she can.

CLAUDIA

Why?

LUIS

My mom made me go to the hospital with them. I was
so annoyed at having to sit there in the waiting room
for hours. But when she put my baby sister in my
arms—she wasn't even an hour old—I . . .

Claudia stops working and stares at Luis. He keeps his eyes
firmly on the pieces.

CLAUDIA

You what?

LUIS

I wasn't mad at my mom anymore. I could see how
much she loved my little sister, and I could see
how much she loved me. She did the best she could.
And that finally seemed like enough.

Claudia smiles.

CLAUDIA

That's really sweet, Luis.

He shrugs, embarrassed.

LUIS

Just tell her to hold the baby.

————

INT. LUIS'S DINING ROOM—LATER

The puzzle is nearly complete. Claudia presses in two pieces, and then there is only one hole left.

Claudia holds up two pieces. One is red and one is green. She takes the red piece and presses it into the final hole in the puzzle.

CLAUDIA

Ta-da!

LUIS (O.S.)

Which leaves one green piece left. Now comes the question . . . is there something written on the back?

Luis zooms in on the piece so it fills the frame.

CLAUDIA

One, two, three.

She flips it over.

A

Horses in a row

From: Claudia Dalton <claudiadalton195@gmail.com>

Date: Monday, July 13, 2015 5:23 PM EST

To: Kate Anderson <kateanderson854@gmail.com>

Subject: All the clues so far . . .

Dear Kate,

    See attached. I've organized all the clues for you.

Claudia

Piece (Front)	Piece (Back)	Letter	Puzzle	Place
Gold—C-3PO's head	Find the time capsule	[none]	Star Wars	??
Black/white dots—stars in the sky	Entrance to Skylab	R	Orbiting Earth	Air and Space Museum
Blue—background behind dinosaur	Horns on Uncle Beazley	I	The Gentle Giant	Natural History Museum
Red—flag	Bobs on the pendulum	B	The Star-Spangled Banner	American History Museum
Green—??	Horses in a row	A	??	??

Claudia Dalton's Cell Phone | Monday, July 13, 2015, 6:05 p.m.

KATE

> Did you get the spreadsheet?

Yeah, thanks
What does the latest clue mean?

> Don't know

Maybe another museum?
An art museum?

> Maybe. There are lots
> of paintings of horses

What do the letters mean?
R, I, B, A

> No clue

Rib, bar, air, bair

> Bair is not a word
> You never were very good at Boggle

Ha ha
Be nice

> I am nice!
> I bought you a present

You did?!

> Well, actually it's for your little brother

No fair!

It's so cute
You're gonna love it
And I have some advice for you too

What?

It's from Luis
He said go to the hospital
when the baby is born

Why?
Boring
Hours of waiting around

Bring a book
Bring a tablet to watch movies
It's summer
You're gonna do the same things at home

So why go?

Be part of it

I don't want to see . . .

Not that!
But Luis held his sister when
she was less than an hour old
Said it made him feel like part of the family

Hmm
Maybe

Luis knows what he's talking about
He changes a mean diaper

Haha
Did he take a class?

Nope

Can he swaddle?

I don't think so

Ha! I'm an expert swaddler

Kate, you're gonna be a great big sister

I hope so

WHILE WE ATE dinner, Papa and I talked about all the places we might find "horses in a row." It had to be another museum, but we'd already visited Air and Space, Natural History, and American History. Maybe this time it was an art museum? The National Gallery of Art. The Hirshhorn. The National Portrait Gallery. We had so much fun talking about it, looking up directions on my phone, it wasn't until I was doing the dishes that I realized we hadn't had an awkward pause at all.

INT. WEST BUILDING OF NATIONAL GALLERY OF ART—DAY
Claudia and Papa stand in front of Renoir's *Girl with a Watering Can*. They each pretend to hold a watering can.

————

INT. WEST BUILDING—LATER
Claudia and Luis stare at Monet's *Japanese Footbridge*.

                    LUIS
      If you were a frog, do you think you could hop on all
      those lily pads?

                    CLAUDIA
      Ribbit.

The camera shakes as Papa laughs.

————

INT. EAST BUILDING OF NATIONAL GALLERY OF ART—DAY
Papa and Luis stare at a modern art painting, paint spattered on a canvas.

                    CLAUDIA (O.S.)
      It's so neat how the colors join together.

                    PAPA
      I could paint that.

Claudia and Luis laugh.

————

INT. EAST BUILDING—LATER

The camera points up at the ceiling. Huge Alexander Calder mobiles sway in the air.

                              LUIS (O.S.)
                    I thought mobiles were for babies.

Claudia giggles.

                              ———

INT. EAST BUILDING—LATER
The camera focuses on a statue of a nude woman.

                              PAPA
                    Look! Another naked lady.

Everyone starts laughing, so hard, Claudia's clutching her stomach.

                          PAPA (CONT'D)
                          (fakely stern)
                    Stop it, you two! That guard's giving us a dirty look.

Luis turns the camera to face the guard.
    The guard is doing his best not to smile.

                              ———

EXT. NATIONAL MALL—DAY
Papa is filming now. Claudia and Luis sit on a bench, each licking a red, white, and blue Popsicle.

                              LUIS
                    Mmm. Artificial colors.

Claudia laughs. Both their mouths are bright red. There is music in the air, like from an old-fashioned organ grinder. Bits of hair that have escaped Claudia's ponytail dance around her eyes in the light breeze.

All at once, Claudia's eyes get really wide. Blue liquid drips down the Popsicle and onto her knee. She doesn't notice.

                         CLAUDIA
          Look!

She points and Papa turns the camera.

A merry-go-round is about fifty feet away. It's brightly colored, with horses going up and down, music playing, kids squealing.

                    CLAUDIA (CONT'D)
          Horses in a row.

                         LUIS
          Let's go on it!

                         CLAUDIA
          Film us, Papa?

Papa is silent for a long moment.

                       PAPA (O. S.)
          No, I want to come too.

Claudia grins as the scene goes black.

[RECORDING BEGINS]

Lily, I rode the merry-go-round today. I rode on a carousel! I don't think I've done that since . . . since I was a tiny boy. It went so fast, I felt dizzy. I want to do it again. I wish you had been there too. I've been so sad these past few months. And then when Jeff left, I felt like a big ball of regret, knotted up with thoughts of what I could have done differently and what I had lost.

But doing this treasure hunt with Claudia, it's like I'm slowly untangling myself, finding the joy in . . .

Ugh, I sound like a greeting card. A sappy greeting card! On the other hand, if I'm feeling better, who cares what I sound like?!

Love you, Lily.

[RECORDING ENDS]

From: Claudia Dalton <claudiadalton195@gmail.com>
Date: Tuesday, July 14, 2015 8:45 PM EST
To: Jeffery Dalton <jeffdalton327@gmail.com>
Subject: Horses in a Row

Oh, Dad, what a great day! Papa, Luis, and I goofed around at the art museum, then we had popsicles, and then I realized the "Horses in a Row" clue was referring to the merry-go-round.

We all went on it, even Papa! It was so much fun. The ride went so fast the wind blew all the hair out of my ponytail. There was an empty horse beside me, and I kept imagining you were there, riding with us.

When we got home, Luis and I found "The County Fair." It had a big carousel on the front, just like the one on the Mall, and another videotape too. The puzzle only had 300 pieces, so we finished it in no time, with one piece left over—a white piece, with one of your clues on the back.

Papa and I are going to watch the videotape now. I like seeing you as a kid. Please come home, so you can go on the merry-go-round with us—for real this time!

Love, Claudia

EXT. NATIONAL MALL—DAY

It's the kite festival. Hundreds of people stand on the lawn in front of the Washington Monument, flying kites. Dragons and butterflies, box kites, and the plain old diamond ones too.

> BRIAN (O.S.)
> Jeff, over here!

Jeff tilts the camera down. Brian is wearing shorts and a T-shirt. He's standing next to a tall man wearing a tight purple T-shirt and blue jeans. The sun glints off a diamond stud in his right ear.

> BRIAN
> This is my uncle Gary. He's visiting from California.

> UNCLE GARY
> You must be Jeff. It's so nice to finally meet you. I brought you boys a present.

He holds up a package: it's a dinosaur kite.

————

EXT. NATIONAL MALL—LATER

Brian and Jeff are holding the assembled kite.

> UNCLE GARY (O.S.)
> Is this thing on?

> JEFF
> Yeah, I can see the red light.

> UNCLE GARY (O.S.)
> Okay, go for it!

Brian runs holding the ball of string. Jeff follows with the kite.

UNCLE GARY (O.S.) (CONT'D)

Now!

Jeff throws the kite into the air. It immediately catches the wind and sails into the sky.

All three of them cheer.

———

EXT. NATIONAL MALL—LATER

The camera focuses on the dinosaur kite while the boys talk off-screen.

JEFF (O.S.)

You're moving?!

BRIAN (O.S.)

Not until summer.

JEFF (O.S.)

But who will I sit with at lunch?

BRIAN (O.S.)

Very funny.

JEFF (O.S.)

I'm serious.

BRIAN (O.S.)

Lunch is serious business.

                    JEFF (O.S.)
I'm gonna miss you.

                    BRIAN (O.S.)
I might miss you too.

                    JEFF (O.S.)
No, you make friends easy. Even Dwight and Jason
don't pick on you.

                    BRIAN (O.S.)
Sure, I get along with people. But it's not easy to
find a good friend. One you want to keep in touch
with.

                    JEFF (O.S.)
Me?

                    BRIAN (O.S.)
You might get a letter or two.

Jeff laughs. The dinosaur kite loops and circles through the air.

                    ————

EXT. NATIONAL MALL—LATER
The merry-go-round sparkles in the sunlight. Uncle Gary and
Brian's little sister are sitting on horses, waiting for the ride to
start. Jeff films them.

                    JEFF (O.S.)
Your family is so cool.

                        BRIAN (O.S.)
No, they aren't.

                        JEFF (O.S.)
Your uncle bought us a kite and is going on the
merry-go-round!

Before Brian can reply, the ride dings and the horses jerk into
motion. Brian's little sister starts to scream. She's suddenly terrified, gripping onto the pole for dear life.

The horses move so fast, we see her crying, then wailing, then
the next time the horses come around, Uncle Gary has climbed off
his horse and is standing beside her.

The next time, she's shaking the reins and laughing, the wind
blowing back her hair.

The ride ends. Uncle Gary helps his niece down. She puts her
hand in his as they walk back to her mother, both grinning.

                        SISTER
I did it!

                     BRIAN'S MOM
That's my brave girl.

The little sister runs off.

                  BRIAN'S MOM (CONT'D)
                    (to Uncle Gary)
You're so good with children.

                     UNCLE GARY
You have awesome kids, sis.

He puts his arm around her and they walk off.

> JEFF (O.S.)
> (to Brian)
> Is your uncle married?

Brian laughs.

> BRIAN (O.S.)
> Jeff, he's gay.

> JEFF (O.S.)
> What?

The screen goes black.

WHEN THE VIDEO ended, Papa muttered, "How could Jeff be so naïve?" I asked him what he meant, and he said, "It was so obvious that guy was . . . not straight."

I turned to him and said you can't tell if someone's gay just because they wear an earring and a purple shirt. And then Papa said, "Maybe not today, but you could in 1987!"

And we got into kind of a fight. Arguing about stereotypes and being naïve like my father, and finally I went to my room and slammed the door.

I'd had a great day with Papa. And now to find out he was so judgmental, well, it made me feel like I didn't really know him at all.

Walter Dalton's Cell Phone | Tuesday, July 14, 2015, 9:34 p.m.

[RECORDING BEGINS]

Lily, I think I messed up tonight. Claudia and I got in a huge fight after watching one of Jeff's home movies. See, one of his old friends from school had a gay uncle, and I made some stupid comment, and she just let me have it. Apparently, she thinks I'm a homophobic jerk!

The thing is, I didn't care if the guy in the video was gay. I was upset because Jeff seemed to admire him in a way Jeff never admired me. You know, Lily, how Jeff and I always struggled to . . . connect, I guess my therapist would say. I asked him to do stuff with me, football and baseball, but he wasn't into those things. Watching these videos, I don't know. I think maybe I should have tried more stuff he was interested in.

And now Claudia's upset! We had such a fun day, working on that silly treasure hunt. She's still working Jeff's puzzles. Claudia's still convinced her dad's going to come home if she finds the prize at the end. Maybe she is as naïve as Jeff . . . but I don't want to make the same mistakes with her.

[RECORDING ENDS]

Pieces of the
Awakening

Claudia Dalton's Cell Phone | Wednesday, July 15, 2015, 8:40 a.m.

KATE

Kate?
You up?

It's summer. Sleeping in

I know. It's just . . .
Another clue from my dad
"Pieces of the Awakening"

Isn't The Awakening some book?

Is it?

I think. BRB

8:50 a.m.

Yeah, by Kate Chopin
Real happy story according to the summary I read

What does it have to do with my dad?

No clue

Hmm
Did you ask your parents about the hospital?

Yeah

And?

They said I can come

Yay!

But if I complain, I have to take the bus home
I'm gonna pack a bag today
Be ready when Mom goes into labor
Junky magazines. Couple of graphic novels.
Granola bars. Charger

Cool

What you doing?

I guess I'm going to the library
to check out *The Awakening*

Good luck

You too

PAPA KEPT HIS nose buried in the paper over breakfast, but he agreed to take me to the library when I asked. In the car, it felt like we had gone back to the beginning of my visit, when everything was awkward. It made me sad, but I didn't know what to say, so I just sat there and was silent.

Claudia Dalton's Cell Phone | Wednesday, July 15, 2015, 4:15 p.m.

Mom: Hi, sweetie!

Claudia: Hi, Mom.

Mom: I'll be home on Friday.

Claudia: I know. Papa and I are planning to come pick you up from the airport.

Mom: Good. Can't wait to see you. I've missed you, honey.

Claudia: Me too. How's your trip been?

Mom: Good. Work stuff went well. And I've had a lot of time to think.

Claudia: About what?

Mom: Just about the future. We can talk when I get home.

Claudia: No, we can talk now. I'm not busy. Just reading this book.

Mom: Claudia, I'm not sure it's appropriate to—

Claudia: Not appropriate? What were you thinking about?!

Mom: [SILENCE]

Claudia: Tell me!

Mom: When we get home, I think I need to call a lawyer.

Claudia: Mom!

Mom: I'm not going to do anything yet. But I was talking to this woman I met at the conference whose husband left her—not disappeared, but . . . The point is, we need to know how to protect ourselves. Figure out what to do if he doesn't—

Claudia: He'll come back!

Mom: I hope so. You deserve better than—

Claudia: Don't say anything bad about Dad!

Mom: Sorry. I didn't want to tell you like this. But I've gone from worried to seriously pissed off. Why is he doing this? Why hasn't he gotten in touch?

Claudia: We've heard from him!

Mom: Claudia, a puzzle piece and a song on your playlist is not "hearing from your father."

Claudia: We just have to find the time capsule.

Mom: And then what?

Claudia: I don't know. Maybe we'll understand.

Mom: Understand what? Why he left?

Claudia: I don't know. But I'm not leaving until we find it.

Mom: Then you'd better do it fast. Because I'm coming back Friday and then we're going home.

From: Claudia Dalton <claudiadalton195@gmail.com>
Date: Wednesday, July 15, 2015 5:27 PM EST
To: Jeffery Dalton <jeffdalton327@gmail.com>
Subject: Clue—Urgent!!

Dear Dad,

I need another clue. Please. Fast. Mom is coming home on Friday and she's . . . upset. I read the book, but I'm sorry, I can't figure it out. And I just have to find this time capsule before I go! I need you to come home.

Love, Claudia

Claudia Dalton's Cell Phone | Thursday, July 16, 2015, 2:47 a.m.

PHONE TRANSCRIPT

Luis: [MUMBLES] Hello?

Claudia: Luis?

Luis: What time is it?

Claudia: 2:47 a.m.

Luis: In the morning?

Claudia: Yeah. I woke you. I shouldn't have called. I'm sorry I—

Luis: No, no, it's okay. You all right?

Claudia: No.

Luis: What's wrong?

Claudia: I don't know.

Luis: Your dad?

Claudia: No, it's my mom. She's going to call a lawyer when she gets home.

Luis: Oh.

Claudia: I mean, it's not like I'm exactly surprised, but . . . he's such a good dad.

Luis: [SILENCE]

Claudia: What if he's just saying good-bye? A real long, drawn-out good-bye. What if we find the time capsule and he still doesn't come home?

Luis: [SILENCE]

Claudia: Say something!

Luis: I don't know what to say.

Claudia: [CRYING]

Luis: Even if he doesn't come back, you'll know a little more about him.

Claudia: What do you mean?

Luis: I mean, you've watched all those videos. And we've gone all these places. Places he went as a kid. We've done the same things.

Claudia: Yeah. Sometimes I could almost imagine he was there with us. That he had ducked out of sight for minute. To get some water or go to the bathroom.

Luis: And isn't that a little bit like finding him?

Claudia: I guess it is. Can I ask you something?

Luis: Sure.

Claudia: What . . . what was the hardest part? When your parents split up?

Luis: [SILENCE]

Claudia: Was it having two houses, or bringing your homework from place to place, or . . .

Luis: [SILENCE]

Claudia: You don't have to answer.

Luis: No, I'm just thinking.

Claudia: Okay.

Luis: I think it was accepting that there was nothing I could do about it. I could work as hard as I wanted at school, and do all my chores without being asked at home, and it still wouldn't make a difference.

Claudia: Oh. So what did you do?

Luis: I had started watching all those documentaries, so I decided to take a film class. I found that I loved it. When you're editing a film, you look at all the clips, all the pieces, and then you have to figure out why and how they fit together.

Claudia: Like a puzzle.

Luis: Yeah, it is like that. Filming makes me feel like I have a little more control over my life.

Claudia: I want that too. Can I watch your movie?

Luis: I haven't finished it yet.

Claudia: Well, let me know when you do. I'd love to see it.

Luis: Really?

Claudia: Of course!

Luis: My mom thinks it's a big waste of time.

Claudia: Well, I don't.

Luis: Thank you, Claudia.

Claudia: No. Thank you. I've never called someone in the middle of the night before. Not even Kate.

Luis: Well, I'm glad you called me. Can you sleep now?

Claudia: I think so.

Luis: Good night, Claudia.

Claudia: Sweet dreams, Luis.

I COULDN'T SLEEP. BUT I felt better. And as I lay in my father's old lumpy bed, I thought about Luis's documentary class and how he was trying to understand all the random bits of everyday life around him. Maybe I could do the same. I liked films. But I liked words even more.

And that was when I came up with the idea for this binder.

NOTE TO READER

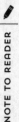

From: Jeffery Dalton <jeffdalton327@gmail.com>

Date: Thursday, July 16, 2015 3:13 AM EST

To: Claudia Dalton <claudiadalton195@gmail.com>

Subject: Last Clue

Potomac Mini Golf at Hains Point

Ohio Dr SW

Washington, DC

I WAS SO EXCITED when I woke up and checked my email. Dad had responded! And the subject line of his email said this was the last clue.

Papa almost spit out his coffee when I showed him the message. I called Luis, and the three of us left for Hains Point right after breakfast.

East Potomac Mini Golf Park

Hole	Par	Player 1 Claudia	Player 2 Luis	Player 3 Papa	Player 4	Player 5
1	2	3	4	2		
2	3	3	2	3		
3	2	2	4	3		
4	2	4	1	2		
5	3	2	3	2		
6	3	1	2	3		
7	2	3	2	4		
8	2	3	5	4		
9	3	2	2	3		
	22	23	25	26		

WE PLAYED A whole round of mini golf, but we didn't find anything! Luckily, the old lady working at the counter when we turned in our clubs overheard Luis and me talking about "the Awakening" and chimed in that the statue had been moved to National Harbor in 2008.

So we jumped back in the car and started to drive.

EXT. NATIONAL HARBOR MARINA—DAY

There's a small man-made beach on the edge of the river. *The Awakening* is a huge metal statue rising up out of the sand. There are five pieces to the statue: a gigantic arm reaching up toward the sky, a massive bearded face with its mouth open, an enormous bent knee, the palm of a giant hand with fingernails as big as dinner plates, and an immense foot with a little toe the size of a man's head.

                    LUIS (O.S.)
        Oh my gosh, it's huge.

Claudia sits down on a bench and pulls off her shoes and socks. Papa glances over at her, then does the same.

                    LUIS (O.S.)
        Go on! I'll film you climbing on it.

Claudia runs off toward the statue. A moment later, Papa follows her out onto the sand.

                    PAPA
        Hot! Hot!

Claudia jumps up to touch the elbow of the arm. Papa walks beneath the bended knee. They both high-five the huge palm and smile at each other.

                    CLAUDIA
        Are we okay?

                    PAPA
        Of course we are.

He gives her a big hug.

EXT. NATIONAL HARBOR MARINA—LATER

Papa is filming now. Claudia and Luis climb onto the giant's face and sit on his cheeks, dangling their feet in between his open teeth.

                    CLAUDIA
          You know what this reminds me of?

                    LUIS
          What?

                    CLAUDIA
          Gulliver's Travels.

                    LUIS
          Never read it. But I saw the movie.

                    CLAUDIA
          You know, the scene where Gulliver wakes up on the
          beach and he's surrounded by the Lilliputians?

                    LUIS
          Yeah.

                    CLAUDIA
          It's kind of like that.

                    LUIS
          Yeah. Only we're the Lilliputians.

                    CLAUDIA
          Exactly.

                    LUIS

     Cool.

They think for a moment.

                    LUIS

     "Pieces of the Awakening." Is there . . . a giant puzzle
     on the list?

Claudia pulls out the list from her pocket and scans it quickly.

                   CLAUIDA

     There are a bunch. "Jack and the Beanstalk." "David
     and Goliath." "The Titans."

                    LUIS

     Oh.

                   CLAUDIA

     But you know what? There's only one called
     Gulliver's Travels.

From: Claudia Dalton <claudiadalton195@gmail.com>

Date: Thursday, July 16, 2015 4:30 PM EST

To: Jeffery Dalton <jeffdalton327@gmail.com>

Subject: Gulliver's Travels

Dear Dad,

We found "The Awakening"! And the puzzle of *Gulliver's Travels*. And the VHS tape labeled "Hains Point."

This is it, right? You'd tell me if it was wrong. Because Mom's coming home tomorrow.

Remember the summer you read that book to me? The other fathers were all at work, but since you're a teacher, you were there. I remember feeling so lucky.

Come. Home. Now.

Love, Claudia

From: Jenny Dalton <jennydalton431@gmail.com>
Date: Thursday, July 16, 2015 4:32 PM EST
To: Claudia Dalton <claudiadalton195@gmail.com>
Subject: Flight info

Claudia,

My flight info is attached to this message. See you soon!

Love, Mom

MOM'S FLIGHT INFO

Depart Friday, July 17, 2015

Geneva, Switzerland (GVA)—Lisbon, Portugal (LIS)

6:30 AM—8:00 AM

Change planes

Lisbon, Portugal (LIS)—Boston, MA (BOS)

10:45 AM—1:20 PM

Boston, MA (BOS)—Washington, DC (DCA)

3:55 PM—5:32 PM

INT. PAPA'S KITCHEN—NIGHT

Luis and Claudia are hard at work on the *"Gulliver's Travels"* puzzle. Papa comes into the room and picks up the box.

> **PAPA**
> Only three hundred pieces? You two should be done in no time.

> **CLAUDIA**
> I hope so. Mom's coming home tomorrow.

> **PAPA**
> How can I help?

> **CLAUDIA**
> Pizza?

> **PAPA**
> I'm on it.

He picks up the phone.

———

INT. PAPA'S KITCHEN—LATER

The pizza box on the counter is empty except for a few discarded crusts, but the puzzle is almost done.

> **CLAUDIA**
> There's only two pieces left.

> **LUIS**
> Let me get a close-up.

He goes to the tripod and zooms in. One piece is the white one with "Pieces of the Awakening" on the back. The other is white and blue and silver.

Claudia looks at the puzzle. There is a hole in a white cloud in the sky over Gulliver. She picks up the white piece and presses it into place. Then she turns over the white and blue and silver piece.

"Uptown" is handwritten in pencil. And beneath that is a large letter X.

                    LUIS (CONT'D)
          What?

                    PAPA
          "Uptown"?

                    CLAUDIA
          He said this was the last clue.

                    PAPA
          That's not even a clue. Uptown is just a location.

                    CLAUDIA
          He said this was the last clue!

                    PAPA
          It's okay. We'll—

                    CLAUDIA
          No, it's not okay. Mom is coming home tomorrow.
          She's going to make me go home. We don't have any
          more time!

                         LUIS
     Wait! Let me see.

Claudia hands him the piece, but instead of looking at the words,
he turns it over to look at the picture. He breaks into a huge
smile.

                      LUIS (CONT'D)
     I know what it is.

                        CLAUDIA
     What?

                         LUIS
     It's the missing piece of R2-D2! From the first puzzle.

                        CLAUDIA
     Of course!

                      _____

INT. PAPA'S KITCHEN—LATER
They have the first *Star Wars* puzzle back on the island now. It's
almost done. Claudia puts the last blue and white and silver piece
into place.

Luis and Papa sit there looking at her.

                         PAPA
     Are there any other pieces?

                        CLAUDIA
     No.

                    LUIS
        I don't understand. It just led back to the beginning.

They all look at each other. No one can figure out what to say.

                LUIS (CONT'D)
        What do we do?

                    CLAUDIA
        I don't know.

WHEN I SNAPPED the final piece into R2-D2, I'm not sure what I expected to happen. A trapdoor to open? A secret audio message to start playing? A map of the time capsule's location to suddenly appear? But I'll tell you what *did* happen.

Absolutely nothing.

I've never been so disappointed in my entire life.

I didn't know what to do. Maybe it was the wrong puzzle. Maybe we were supposed to do one of the giant ones after all. But it didn't matter. We were out of time.

And then I remembered. We hadn't watched the video labeled "Hains Point."

EXT. MINI GOLF—DAY

A bunch of boys are standing at the mini golf counter, picking out putters.

>   PAPA (O.S.)
>   Smile, boys!

The boys turn to look at the camera. Jeff is standing next to Brian, who slaps a third boy on the back.

>   BRIAN
>   Happy birthday, Jason!

———

EXT. HAINS POINT PARK—DAY

Hains Point is a big, open park on the Potomac River. There are half-eaten plates of cake discarded on a picnic table. Behind the table, *The Awakening* rises out of mulch. The group of boys from mini golf play on the enormous hands and face.

The camera watches the boys for a moment, then turns up to the sky. A plane flies overhead, low as it approaches the airport. For a moment, the roar of the engines overpowers everything else.

But once the plane is gone, we can hear someone screaming.

The camera whips back around to the statue. Jeff is on the ground, next to the huge metal head, clutching his wrist.

>   PAPA (O.S.)
>   Jeff!

He runs toward his son, forgetting the camera is still recording. The next dialogue is heard over a view of mulch.

                    PAPA (O.S.) (CONT'D)
What happened?

                    BRIAN (O.S.)
Dwight pushed him!

                    DWIGHT (O.S.)
I didn't mean . . . I barely touched him!

                    BRIAN (O.S.)
You called him a—

                    JEFF (O.S.)
Oww!

More scrambling. We catch a glimpse of Jeff on the ground as the
camera swings forgotten on his father's arm.

                    PAPA (O.S.)
Call an ambulance!

                    BRIAN (O.S.)
You're gonna be okay. It's fine.

The camera swings again. Brian is kneeling on the ground next
to Jeff, his hand on his uninjured arm.

                    PAPA (O.S.)
Stupid thing is still on.

The screen goes black.

Then I felt even worse. The video didn't help. My father never mentioned he had broken his wrist. I guess there were a lot of things I didn't know about him.

Luis went home, Papa went to bed early, and I sat there in the kitchen. Just sat there, thinking about how much I hated my father.

[RECORDING BEGINS]

Oh, Lily. You should have seen her face. She was so disappointed. We did the last puzzle and . . . nothing.

The thing is, even if we didn't find anything . . . it was fun. I really had fun with Claudia. And watching those videos, yeah, sure it's been painful. But, oh gosh, I wish I had taken more. I can't get enough of them. And that was all Claudia too. I would have dumped them in the trash without her.

I know Claudia thought following these clues would help her find her father again. But remembering all those things, all those nice memories—her watching the videos and learning all those new things about him—it's kind of like we already did.

I hope I can help her see that. I'm too tired to try now. All that driving and walking. Can't keep up with a couple of twelve-year-olds. But maybe tomorrow. I miss you.

[RECORDING ENDS]

Claudia Dalton's Cell Phone | Thursday, July 16, 2015, 10:15 p.m.

KATE

What happened? Did you find it?

No

[missed call from Kate]

What happened?!

It didn't lead anywhere
Sorry, too frustrated to talk

Oh my gosh, I'm so sorry!
Let me know if there is anything I can do

Claudia Dalton's Cell Phone | Friday, July 17, 2015, 12:04 a.m.

MOM

I'm boarding my plane in a minute
Know you're probably asleep, but
I just wanted to say I love you
See you later today!

Claudia: Hello?

Luis: Claudia?

Claudia: What?

Luis: I can't sleep.

Claudia: Neither can I.

Luis: I don't understand.

Claudia: I don't either!

Luis: [SILENCE]

Claudia: I'm sorry, Luis. I don't mean to be grumpy. It's just . . .

Luis: I know. I'm exhausted too. Let's talk in the morning.

Claudia: Okay. I really appreciate your help.

Luis: I know. Sweet dreams, Claudia.

INT. PAPA'S KITCHEN—NIGHT

The camera films the empty kitchen. It's dark and late. Claudia walks into the frame. Her eyes are red as if she's been crying.

>   CLAUDIA
>   It's 1:17 a.m. and I can't sleep and I'm making this
>   video for you, Dad. Just to tell you how much I hate
>   you. You tricked me! Just like Obi-Wan tricked the
>   Stormtroopers.

She gestures to the puzzle.

>   CLAUDIA (CONT'D)
>   It was all just a stupid game, wasn't it? Even if it
>   had led to a time capsule, how would that ever have
>   anything to do with where you are now?! I'm such
>   an idiot!

She picks up the puzzle and crumples it in her hands. The pieces break apart easily, like crushing cornflakes in a bowl. Claudia takes the pieces and throws them everywhere, throwing as hard as she can, until they're scattered all over the kitchen.

Then she puts her head down on the island and starts to sob. The TV, left on in the background, drones on as she cries.

INT. GYM—DAY

A smiling man and woman in workout clothes pose in front of a sleek-looking treadmill.

>   MAN
>   The EXERPRO 2000 is a piece of exercise equiptment
>   like no other. No longer will you envy others with
>   their fit bodies.

>   WOMAN
>   And there's no long hours at the gym either. From the
>   comfort of your own home, you can use the EXERPRO
>   2000 to transform your body—and your life!

WHEN I WOKE up the next morning, I was still in the kitchen, my face pressed against the island. The sun was shining through the open blinds, directly into my eyes.

I sat up and realized there was a puzzle piece stuck to my cheek. Carefully, as if removing a Band-Aid, I peeled it off.

It was a standard puzzle piece. With two pockets and two tabs. Gold. Probably part of C-3PO. I twirled the piece in my fingers, staring at it. The piece was so old, there were cracks in the cardboard on the back. Lots of cracks. They looked like lines.

No, wait.

They *were* lines. Pencil lines.

I was suddenly wide-awake. I scrambled around on the table, reaching for more pieces. There were two within hand's reach. The first had nothing on its back. Just the cardboard, gray and faded with age.

The second had more pencil lines. As if someone had drawn them there on purpose.

I jumped up and switched on the overhead light, picking up the pieces, putting them into the lid of the box. One of them had a small *N* on it with an arrow pointing up. As if it were a compass rose. As if it were part of a map!

I searched under breakfast bar stools, under the TV, flipped through the recycling. One piece was in my tennis shoe, cuddled up under the tongue.

I dumped the pieces onto the table and started working. When I was done, Luke, the droids, Obi-Wan, and the Stormtroopers stared back at me.

I went to the recycling bin again and found an old cereal box. I ripped it open to make a huge cardboard spatula and slipped it carefully under the puzzle, turning it over.

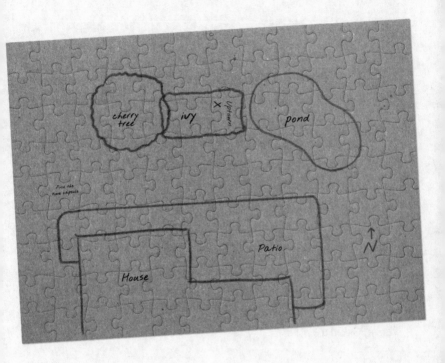

From: Claudia Dalton <claudiadalton195@gmail.com>
Date: Friday, July 17, 2015 6:48 AM EST
To: Jeffery Dalton <jeffdalton327@gmail.com>
Subject: The Map

Dear Dad,

I can't believe it. I thought . . .

Last night, when I couldn't sleep, I thought about the time I had the flu and you stayed up all night with me. We watched one infomercial after another, electric grills and blenders and jewelry and exercise equipment. The actors were all so happy, so sure their product would solve all our problems! I guess I kind of thought finding the time capsule would be like that.

I know that's stupid. Still, I wanted so much to find it. And now I think I have! Drawn on the back of the very first puzzle. Nana and Papa's backyard, with the cherry tree and the fishpond and an X marking the spot.

It's almost 7:00 a.m. Late enough to wake Luis up, I think. And Papa. We have some digging to do.

Love, Claudia

PART 3

The Big Picture

SO NOW COMES the part we've all been waiting for. Here's how we found the time capsule.

Claudia Dalton's Cell Phone | Friday, July 17, 2015, 7:01 a.m.

Luis: Hello?

Claudia: Come over now.

Luis: What?

Claudia: Come over now!

Luis: What time is it?

Claudia: 7:02 a.m.

Luis: It's too early.

Claudia: It's important. I found the map.

Luis: Map?

Claudia: To the time capsule!

Luis: What?!

Claudia: Come over.

Luis: On my way.

EXT. PAPA'S BACKYARD—MORNING

The sun is shining, melting the ice in a pitcher of lemonade on the picnic table. The camera is on a tripod with a wide view of the backyard. There's ivy, grass, an empty fishpond, and a cherry tree, just like on the puzzle map. Claudia and Luis are standing in the ivy between the pond and the tree.

They're both digging with old spades and have been for a while. Claudia's face is red, and wisps of hair, escaped from her ponytail, stick to her cheeks and forehead. Luis takes the hem of his shirt and uses it to wipe the sweat from his face.

                    LUIS
Where's your grandfather?

                    CLAUDIA
Doughnut run.

They both look at the hole they're digging. It's about two feet deep and maybe four feet wide. Luis kicks at the loose dirt they've piled around the hole, making sure they haven't missed anything. He sighs.

                    LUIS
I'm gonna get some lemonade.

                    CLAUDIA
Pour me a glass.

She puts her foot on the shovel and leans her weight onto it. There's a loud clank.

                    CLAUDIA (CONT'D)
Oh!

Luis turns back to look at her.

CLAUDIA (CONT'D)

I think I found something!

They both kneel and begin pawing through the dirt with their hands. After a moment, a corner of a white box appears, sticking out of the dirt. They keep digging and uncover a black handle. Claudia grasps the handle and pulls as hard as she can. With a loud slurp, the box finally breaks free of the clay earth and Claudia falls back into the dirt.

Luis offers her a hand and helps her up. They're both filthy, dirt on their knees and hands, smudged on their sweaty faces. Together, they lift the white metal box onto the picnic table.

The box is about the size of a briefcase. Luis brushes off a chunk of dirt to reveal a sticker that reads *SAFE4EVER—Waterproof & Fireproof Box*. Next to the handle is a five-letter, alphabetic combination lock.

LUIS

What's the code?

CLAUDIA

I have no idea.

From: Claudia Dalton <claudiadalton195@gmail.com>
Date: Friday, July 17, 2015 9:45 AM EST
To: Jeffery Dalton <jeffdalton327@gmail.com>
Subject: The Box

Dear Dad,

    We found the time capsule, but it's locked! Please, Dad, I'm tired.
Mom will be home in a couple of hours. Just send me the code.
Love, Claudia

Claudia Dalton's Cell Phone | Friday, July 17, 2015, 9:55 a.m.

KATE

Kate, we found the time capsule, but we can't open it
It has an alphabet lock
26 letters. Five positions
Papa says that's 26 to the 5th power
11,881,376 possibilities

Why send you clues if you can't open the box?

I know!!
It doesn't make sense

What are you doing now?

Just eating doughnuts

Yummy
Remember how you used to bite
into doughnuts to make a letter C?

Oh

What?

The letters!

What letters?

The letters on the puzzle pieces.
We didn't know what they meant

Oh!

I'm going to send you
a pic of all the pieces

Find the time capsule

R

Entrance to Skylab

Horns on Uncle Beazley

I

Bobs on the pendulum

B

A

Horses in a row

Pieces of the Awakening

N

Uptown

X

Claudia Dalton's Cell Phone | Friday, July 17, 2015, 10:21 a.m.

Claudia: Hi, Kate. You're on speaker. Luis and Papa are here too.

Luis: Hey, Kate.

Papa: Katie-pie!

Kate: Hi, guys.

Claudia: We've got the pieces. I think the letters on the corners must be the code for the combination.

Kate: But there are six letters, and you said it was five-letter code.

Luis: I don't think the *X* counts. That was "X marks the spot." We already used that one.

Claudia: So that leaves five letters: *R-I-B-A-N*.

Kate: Did you try that?

Claudia: Yes. Didn't work in that order.

Papa: Even with only five letters, there are 119 more possibilities.

Claudia: We don't have time to try them all. Mom will be back at 5:32 tonight!

Luis: We need to think. Your dad sent the letters; maybe he sent the order too.

Kate: Question—how many horns *were* on Uncle Beazley?

Luis: Three. He was a triceratops.

Kate: And how many pieces of *The Awakening* were there?

Luis: I don't know. Four?

Claudia: No, there were five. Head, foot, hand, arm, knee.

Kate: So what if the *I* on the Uncle Beazley clue was the third letter? And maybe the *N* from the *Awakening* clue is letter five?

Claudia: Kate, you're a genius!

Papa: I'm an old man. I need to write this down. So you're saying the clue is: "Blank, blank, *I*, blank, *N*."

Kate: Yes.

Claudia: We just need to fill in the other blanks.

Kate: And there's only one bob on a pendulum, so *B* must be the first letter.

Papa: So, "*B*, blank, *I*, blank, *N*." Two left.

Luis: The entrance to Skylab was on the second floor. I remember because I kept looking over the railing to see if there was anyone who might be your father. So *R* is the second letter.

Claudia: And there were four horses in a row on the merry-go-round. Which makes *A* letter number four.

Papa: *B-R-I-A-N.*

[LONG PAUSE]

Kate: "Brian"?

Claudia: It sounds familiar.

Luis: Uncle? Cousin? Friend?

Claudia: Friend! Papa, wasn't Brian the name of Dad's friend in those old home movies?

Papa: Yes, yes, it was!

Kate: Why did he pick his name for the code?

Claudia: Only one way to find out.

EXT. PAPA'S BACKYARD—DAY

Claudia sits in front of the white box on the picnic table. Papa hovers behind her. Luis is filming. Slowly, Claudia brushes the last of the dirt off the lock and begins to turn the letters.

B. R. The third dial is a little stiff, but she manages to turn it. *I. A.* Her fingertips are sweaty, slipping as she tries to turn the final dial. She goes past it at first, all the way to *O.* Then she turns it back one. *N.*

Papa takes a deep breath. Luis takes a step closer.

LUIS (O.S.)

You ready?

Claudia nods and flicks open the lock. The top pops up. Luis walks around the table so that the camera can also see into the box. There's a pile of papers.

LUIS (O.S.) (CONT'D)

Is there a mixtape?

CLAUDIA

No. Just a bunch of papers.

PAPA

What are they?

Dear Parents of 7th Grade Students
at George Washington Junior High:

All 7th grade science classes will be taking a field trip
to the Air and Space Museum on Friday, September 26,
1986. Buses will leave the school promptly at 9:00 a.m. and
return by 1:30 p.m.

The groups for Mrs. Johnson's class are as follows:

Group 1
Latonya Gayles
Carla Gray
Amanda Vanderweele
Tracey Harper

Group 4
Steve Dunlow
Keith Poretz
Jerome McDonald
Thomas Sharpe

Group 2
Paul Craven
Tony Palmer
Sean McQueen
James Fitch

Group 5
Karen Rivers
Suzanne Evans
Elizabeth Ferguson
Anne White

Group 3
Jeff Dalton
Brian Tuckerman
Dwight Griffin
Jason Lewis

Group 6
Sara Wyatt
Brandon Cooper
Darrell Carter
Crystal Holmes

Educational Department

DINOLAB— BEHIND THE SCENES!!

In this four-week program, go behind the scenes with real scientists as they work on fossils at the Smithsonian "DINOLAB."

....

SAT   1:00–4:00 PM
Start Date: 2/7/87

$150 Smithsonian Associate Members
$200 Non-Members

George Washington Junior High School Achievement Award

Certificate of Excellence

THIS CERTIFICATE IS PRESENTED TO:

JEFF DALTON & BRIAN TUCKERMAN

BY THE *ADMINISTRATION* AND *FACULTY*
IN RECOGNITION OF OUTSTANDING ACCOMPLISHMENT AND
PERFORMANCE IN THE ALEXANDRIA JR./SR. HIGH SCHOOL
SCIENCE FAIR FOR YOUR PROJECT ON:

THE PERIOD OF A PENDULUM

SIGNED THIS TWENTY-FIRST DAY OF MARCH 1987

_____
Evelyn Bates TEACHER / SPONSOR

_____
Robert Howard PRINCIPAL

Smithsonian

KITE FESTIVAL

Saturday, March 28, 1987

Come bring a kite and participate in events on and around the National Mall. If we're lucky, the cherry blossoms may be in bloom as well!!

You're Invited!
Jason's 13th Birthday

WHAT: _Please join us for cake and mini golf_

WHEN: _Saturday, April 18, 1987_

WHERE: _Hains Point Golf Course_

TIME: 2:00—5:00 PM

RSVP: 703-555-4936

UPTOWN 1
STAR WARS

★ ★ ★ ★ ★

1502 $5.00   5/23/87

003438 TC 2 5

003438 TC 2 5

EXT. PAPA'S BACKYARD—CONTINUOUS

Papa points into the box.

> PAPA
>
> There's one more thing.

Claudia pulls an envelope out of a pocket on the top of the metal safe. Luis zooms in. On the front of the envelope it says "To Brian."

> CLAUDIA
>
> Should I open it?

> LUIS
>
> He sent you the clues to find it.

Claudia looks at Papa. He nods.

> PAPA
>
> Go ahead.

Claudia runs her fingertips over the words, then rips the envelope open. There are six sheets of notebook paper, covered with writing.

> CLAUDIA
>
> I'll read it to you.

She clears her throat. Luis adjusts the camera so that it's focusing on her face.

> CLAUDIA (CONT'D)
>
> "May 24, 1987. Dear Brian, It's almost three in the morning and I can't stop crying. I'm just gonna die if

I don't tell someone, even if it's just you in this letter,
which I am never going to send. I can't sleep anyway.
I'm so sorry I messed everything up. We were having
such a good time at the movies. I'm so sorry I had to
ruin it all by . . ."

Claudia's stops reading. Her mouth hangs half-open.

                    LUIS
    Go on.

Her eyes are still scanning the letter, but she doesn't say a word.

                  CLAUDIA
    Stop the camera.

                    PAPA
    What does it say? What is he sorry about?!

Claudia shakes her head.

                  CLAUDIA
    Stop filming!

The screen goes black.

May 24, 1987

Dear Brian,

It's almost three in the morning and I can't stop crying. I'm just gonna die if I don't tell someone, even if it's just you in this letter, which I am never going to send. I can't sleep anyway. I'm so sorry I messed everything up. We were having such a good time at the movies. I'm so sorry I had to ruin it all by trying to kiss you.

I have to get it out of my head. So I never have to think about it again. I will never think about it again. But I have to explain. To you. To myself. It's not like I planned it. It wasn't a date or anything. I just wanted to see my favorite movie with my best friend.

We had so much fun laughing and joking in the car on the way there. No one can make me laugh as hard as you. And then, when we were in the theater and the Star Wars music started playing and you smiled at me, I got this horrible, awful, wonderful feeling. Like a cramp in my stomach from too much Mountain Dew and my heart was fluttering from all the caffeine. But I hadn't had any soda and I didn't have the flu.

And I just felt so happy. Like it didn't matter that Dwight and Jason call me names at school. Or that Dad is bugging me to join the football team again. It didn't even matter that you're leaving in two weeks. Because in that moment, everything in the world was absolutely right. Absolutely perfect. Like I couldn't ever get any happier.

I looked over at you as the escape pod fell to Tatooine and I could see your face in the glow of the two suns and you looked as happy as I felt. And you glanced over at me and you smiled, and then you put your arm on the armrest so it was touching mine.

It was touching mine!

After that, I couldn't concentrate on the movie at all. I just kept thinking about how your arm was right next to mine. You had on that same striped shirt you'd worn at the beginning at

Skylab. Even in the darkness of the theater, I could make out a few freckles on your arm, just above your wrist. Like stars in the sky.

And then I had a thought.

Maybe you liked me too.

I mean, I know you like me. But maybe you liked me. And you are moving in two weeks. And what if you liked me and I never knew because I never told you.

Then Obi-wan was using the Jedi mind trick on the Stormtroopers. I always loved that scene. I'd gotten a puzzle of it one year at Christmas. And I thought, I'll try it on Brian. Maybe I can get him to smile at me again.

I know, it sounds insane. I know there's no Jedi mind trick and you can't will someone to do something just by thinking it. But for some reason, it seemed completely logical at the time. Like, yes, of course, that's an excellent plan.

So I started thinking, Look over at me and smile. Look over at me and smile. Again and again and again. While Alderaan blew up, and Luke released

Leia from her cell, and they all escaped the trash compactor.

Then just before Luke and Leia swung across the chasm in the Death Star, it happened. You turned to look at me and smiled.

And that's when I leaned over . . .

I don't know what I was thinking! I didn't know what I was going to do. I didn't even get close to your mouth. But when you put your hands up and pushed me away and asked, "What the hell, dude? Are you trying to kiss me?!!" I honestly thought I was going to die.

My lungs tightened and I couldn't breathe. There was this horrible ringing in my ears. While Darth Vader killed Obi-Wan, I kept blinking, blinking, but I couldn't make my eyes focus. I was hot, then cold, then hot again, my heart pounding with the music. You leaned over to the other side of your seat, as far away from me as possible. I felt like I was going to throw up.

I wasn't planning to kiss you! It was just an

impulsive thing. And kids are impulsive, right? It didn't mean anything. I'm not like your uncle, I'm really not. I mean, sure, maybe I've thought about kissing a guy before, but it was just a thought. I bet a lot of guys think about that. They just don't talk about it because it's too embarrassing. It doesn't mean . . . anything!

Okay, so maybe part of me would like to be like your uncle. I don't want an earring, but I'd love to be as brave as him, and not care about what anyone says about how I dress or act. But I'm not like that. Except when I'm around you, Brian. You make me feel brave and confident and like myself. I'm sorry I had to go and ruin our friendship.

I wish I had been fearless enough to say some of that to you. But I wasn't. We just sat there and watched Luke blow up the Death Star and I wanted to be on it too. You are brave, and I know you were trying to be nice when you wanted to talk to me about what had happened afterward. But . . . I don't want to talk about it.

I never want to talk about it. I just want to forget it ever happened. Those feelings didn't mean anything, and if I ever have them again, I just need to ignore them. Maybe I was trying to kiss you—I don't know—but it doesn't matter, because nothing like that is ever going to happen again.

I'm glad you're moving. Glad in two weeks you're going to leave and I'll never see you again. No one can ever know what I did. No one. I should burn this letter as soon as I'm done writing it.

But I can't. I just can't. I can't erase our friendship. That's all it was, right? A friendship. I will be different. I'll be good. I won't have these thoughts anymore. I won't let myself.

But I don't want to forget.

Your friend forever,
Jeff

YOU'RE PROBABLY WONDERING how I felt in those first few moments after I read my dad's letter to Brian. I'd like to tell you something really dramatic happened. Like I started screaming or crying or smashed the pitcher of lemonade against the wall.

But really, I just sat there thinking, *Wow, my father really wanted to kiss that boy.* Even though he'd spent most of the letter telling us he didn't, I didn't believe him for one second. It was obvious . . . he'd liked him and wanted to kiss him.

My father had wanted to kiss a boy?!

What did that mean? Why had he wanted me to read that letter? Was my dad . . . gay?

That was crazy. Why did he marry my mom if he wanted to be with a guy? I mean, just last month, the Supreme Court had decided . . .

Just last month. And Mom and Dad had gotten married years and years ago. In 1999.

Papa wanted to read the letter then, so I handed it to him. Luis asked what it said, but I couldn't answer. I kept waiting to feel angry or sad or something. But my thoughts just kept spinning.

Was this the thing he had to think about? Was this the thing he couldn't bring himself to tell us? Was this why he left?

He'd known the letter was there. He'd wanted me to find it. He'd sent me clues.

My eyes suddenly stung like they did when Kate and I spent all afternoon at the pool without our goggles. And I did feel angry—because it seemed like my dad had left us rather than let us see who he really was.

EXT. PAPA'S BACKYARD—DAY

Papa sits at the picnic table, staring at the cherry tree as if he were watching a small child climbing in its branches.

> LUIS (O.S.)
>
> Are you sure you're okay?

> CLAUDIA (O.S.)
>
> Yeah.

> LUIS (O.S.)
>
> All right. Well, the camera's rolling. I'm gonna go home and take a shower. Call me later?

> CLAUDIA (O.S.)
>
> Okay.

Claudia walks into the frame and sits down next to Papa. He doesn't look at her. Doesn't acknowledge that she's there.

> CLAUDIA (CONT'D)
>
> Papa?

> PAPA
>
> Hmm?

> CLAUDIA
>
> Do you hate Dad now?

He finally turns to look at her.

> PAPA
>
> What?

                    CLAUDIA

Do you hate Dad now?

                     PAPA

No! Why would you say—

                    CLAUDIA

That letter . . . Dad *liked* that boy.

                     PAPA

Yeah.

                    CLAUDIA

So do you hate him?

                     PAPA

Of course not!

                    CLAUDIA

But when we watched that video with Brian's uncle,
you said—

                     PAPA

I say a lot of stupid things.

He turns his gaze back to the tree. Claudia looks too, trying to see
what he's seeing. Her eyes get wide and watery as she stares, but
there's nothing there. Finally, she covers her face with her hands.

                 PAPA (CONT'D)

Are you all right, Claudia?

Claudia shrugs, her face still hidden.

CLAUDIA

(muffled)

I don't know. It's kinda confusing.

PAPA

Yeah. It is.

Papa puts his arm around her. She wipes at her eyes.

CLAUDIA

I mean, I support equal rights for everyone! But . . . I liked my family how it was. I don't want my dad to be gay! And that makes me feel like a bad person. That means I am a bad person, right?!

PAPA

Of course you're not a bad person! You're just surprised.

CLAUDIA

Yeah, I guess. [PAUSE] Do you think that's why he left?

PAPA

I don't know.

CLAUDIA

I hate not knowing!

PAPA

Me too.

They sit there in silence for a long moment.

CLAUDIA

Papa, what are we going to do?

PAPA

I wish I knew.

Walter Dalton's Cell Phone | Friday, July 17, 2015, 12:35 p.m.

[RECORDING BEGINS]

Lily, Lily, I . . . I don't know if I can even say this. Claudia found Jeff's time capsule and there was a letter inside and . . . I think maybe our son is gay.

Did you know? You said something once when he was a kid and . . . and . . . I just said he needed to play more sports. Why didn't you say anything? Why didn't you tell me?!

[RECORDING ENDS]

Kate: Huh.

Claudia: What do you think?

Kate: I don't know.

Claudia: Do you want me to read the letter to you again?

Kate: No. I just don't know what to say, Claudia. It seems so . . .

Claudia: Do you think he's gay?

Kate: I don't know. Maybe he likes both. Boys and girls.

Claudia: So then why leave? What's the problem? If he liked both and was happy with Mom, he wouldn't have left.

Kate: So you think he is?

Claudia: I don't know. Maybe.

[NOISE IN THE BACKGROUND]

Kate: Sorry, hold on a second.

[PAUSE]

Kate: I'm so sorry! I gotta go. My mom's water just broke.

Claudia: What?! She's in labor?

Kate: I think. We're going to the hospital now.

Claudia: Okay. Good luck!

Kate: You too.

INT. KITCHEN—NIGHT

Dad's forty-first birthday party video again. The room is full of people. Streamers hang from the ceiling. Balloons are tied to one chair.

Dad sits in the balloon chair. He's chatting with Kate and her mom.

                    MOM (O.S.)
     Time for cake!

The lights suddenly go out.

Mom walks into the frame, carrying a round cake with two number candles, 4 and 1, on the top. Dad blows out the candles and everyone cheers.

Mom leans in to kiss him. At the last moment, Dad turns his head ever so slightly away, so that her lips graze his cheek instead of his mouth.

                    MOM (CONT'D)
     Happy birthday, sweetie.

Walter Dalton's Cell Phone | Friday, July 17, 2015, 1:21 p.m.

[RECORDING BEGINS]

I'm so angry. How could he have kept this from us? Why did he think we wouldn't understand? What about Jenny?! Has he been lying to her? What did she know?

[RECORDING ENDS]

INT. CHURCH—DAY

The wedding video again. The pastor clears his throat.

PASTOR

Do you, Jeffery Robert Dalton, take Jennifer Ann
Thompson to be your lawfully wedded husband?

Everyone laughs.

LUIS ONCE TOLD me that he loves rewatching his favorite
movies, because every time he does, he sees something different. "The picture doesn't change," he said. "But you do."

Walter Dalton's Cell Phone | Friday, July 17, 2015, 2:14 p.m.

[RECORDING BEGINS]

Lily, remember how I used to say I didn't know a single homosexual? Well, I've been thinking. When I was a kid, there was this old woman on the corner. She rented out a room to her "best friend" for years. We called them both old spinsters, but . . .

And I had a buddy from the service. Handsome as all get-out. Confirmed bachelor. Whenever anyone asked him why he had never settled down, wondered if he just hadn't ever met the right woman, he'd give this wry little smile and say, "Something like that." I wonder now if what he meant was, he'd never met the right man.

It's so strange, Lily. Maybe Jeff wasn't the one who was so naïve—maybe it was me.

[RECORDING ENDS]

Luis: Hey.

Claudia: Hi.

Luis: Just checking on you. You doing okay?

Claudia: I guess. [PAUSE] Can I ask you a personal question?

Luis: Shoot.

Claudia: Do you like girls? I mean, *like* girls. I know we're not even thirteen yet, but ...

Luis: I like girls.

Claudia: You sure?

Luis: Yeah.

Claudia: And you read the letter. Would you ever write to a boy like—

Luis: No!

Claudia: Oh.

Luis: Would you write to a girl that way?

Claudia: I don't think I would. I mean, Kate's my best friend and we're super close, but ... no. [PAUSE] Do you think my dad is gay?

Luis: So what if he is? Even in the little town where my dad and I live, there's a girl in my class with two dads.

Claudia: Was she adopted?

Luis: I think.

Claudia: So that's all she's ever known.

Luis: And there's a boy a grade below me. Both his moms always come to all his basketball games. One of his moms was married before. To a man. I guess I never really thought about his dad before. Or what happened to him. But my point is, no one really cares anymore!

Claudia: I care! And I bet my mom will too.

Luis: Why do you care?

Claudia: Because . . . because my dad is someone different from who I thought he was. I mean, he's the same, but he's different too . . . and it's just so confusing!

Luis: I'm so sorry, Claudia. I wish there was something I could do.

Claudia: Do you think my parents are going to get divorced?

Luis: I don't know. But honestly, things have been better for me since my parents split up. They finally stopped arguing!

Claudia: But my parents didn't argue. Even when Dad disappeared, I thought he'd come home and they'd work out their issues. I thought everything was okay. When everything seems one way—and then suddenly it all changes—what do you do?

[LONG PAUSE]

Luis: I think you just have to trust that you can handle it.

Claudia: But what if I can't?

Luis: I'm not saying it isn't hard. And I'm not saying I know what you should do. But . . . it's like all those puzzles.

Claudia: What do you mean?

Luis: Look at how many times you thought you had come to a dead end. And you figured it out! Every time. You never gave up.

Claudia: Oh. You're right.

Luis: 'Course I am. I'm always right.

Claudia: [GIGGLES]

[NOISE IN THE BACKGROUND]

Claudia: Papa's calling. I gotta go. It's time to pick up my mom.

Luis: Good luck.

Claudia: Thanks, Luis.

INT. RONALD REAGAN WASHINGTON NATIONAL AIRPORT—DAY
Papa is filming on his phone. The arrival screen flickers: American
2119, Boston, 5:32 PM, on time.

The camera tilts down to reveal Claudia, standing as close as
she can to the rope that marks the end of the secure zone. She's
showered since the digging, and is now wearing a sundress and
sandals. Her hair is down, not in its usual ponytail, and she keeps
twisting a lock of it around her index finger. She stares at the people exiting security, scanning the crowd for a familiar face.

All at once, her mouth opens a little and she bounces on her
toes. Then she waves like crazy!

Papa turns the camera to see Mom walking toward them. She's
wearing a suit with old white tennis shoes. She has a computer bag
in one hand and a big purse with heels sticking out the top in the
other. Her hair is pulled back in a ponytail, and she looks tired—
until she sees her daughter, and then all the fatigue drains away
and she smiles.

Mom drops her bags and runs toward Claudia. They hug each
other like a three-year-old and her mother after the first day of
preschool.

When they pull apart, Claudia takes a deep breath. She says
something, but the phone doesn't catch her words. Claudia hands
her mother the envelope.

The screen goes black.

I'D LIKE TO tell you how I felt as I waited for my mother to get off her plane, I really would, but I can't seem to figure out how to squish all those feelings into words I could type onto this page.

I remember I felt cold, and there was a little rock in my right sandal. I'd put the letter back in its envelope and rubbed my finger back and forth over the open flap until I gave myself a paper cut.

I don't remember what words I used when I handed it to her. I do remember sitting in baggage claim, watching the suitcases and backpacks, strollers and duffel bags go around and around on the luggage carousel as she read it.

We stopped at a diner for burgers on the way home. It was very quiet. We passed the letter back and forth until there was ketchup and mustard and grease smudged along its edges.

Then my phone dinged. Guess who it was . . .

Claudia Dalton's Cell Phone | Friday, July 17, 2015, 6:45 p.m.

DAD

Did you find the letter?

Yes

We have a lot to talk about

Yeah
Where are you?

Staying with an old friend, Amanda
In Reading, PA
I'll be home next week
We can talk then

OK

Did Mom get back?

Yes

Love to you both

I N CASE YOU'RE wondering, it was actually Mom typing those responses to Dad. She, Papa, and I were gathered around the little screen of my phone like it was the Super Bowl halftime show and the electricity had just gone out.

I think it was the "Love to you both" comment that made Mom the angriest.

In any case, after that, Mom threw down the phone and was like, "Oh, no! Enough of this being patient. Enough of his games. It's my timeline now. I'm not waiting until next week to see if he happens to follow through on his promise to come home.

"We're going to drive up there and find him. Have a conversation. In person! Not via text. Not on the phone. After fifteen years of marriage, he owes me that!"

Papa and I just stared at her for a minute. Dad wasn't the only one who had changed. It had only been two weeks, but Mom seemed tougher. Stronger. I felt like I suddenly didn't know her either.

I thought about what Luis had said about trusting that you could handle change. It seemed like this new Mom could. And I was a little bit afraid and a little bit impressed.

Papa muttered something about not having the address, but Mom dismissed his concerns with a wave. "We have a name, a city, and Google. It's like he wants us to find him! Think you can handle it, Claudia?"

I nodded. It seemed Mom trusted me too. And I wasn't going to let her down.

Dear Parents of 7th Grade Students
at George Washington Junior High:

All 7th grade science classes will be taking a field trip
to the Air and Space Museum on Friday, September 26,
1986. Buses will leave the school promptly at 9:00 a.m. and
return by 1:30 p.m.

The groups for Mrs. Johnson's class are as follows:

Group 1	**Group 4**
Latonya Gayles	Steve Dunlow
Carla Gray	Keith Poretz
Amanda Vanderweele	Jerome McDonald
Tracey Harper	Thomas Sharpe

Group 2	**Group 5**
Paul Craven	Karen Rivers
Tony Palmer	Suzanne Evans
Sean McQueen	Elizabeth Ferguson
James Fitch	Anne White

Group 3	**Group 6**
Jeff Dalton	Sara Wyatt
Brian Tuckerman	Brandon Cooper
Dwight Griffin	Darrell Carter
Jason Lewis	Crystal Holmes

A s LUCK WOULD have it, Amanda had an unusual last name. So with her city, it only took me a minute to find her. She even had her own website!

Amanda Vanderweele-Blume
Mom Blogger Extraordinaire

Loving Mom to Five Beautiful Children, Amber, 10, Sage, 8, Ash, 5, Ginger, 3, and the baby, Rose, who is almost one. My husband's a long-haul trucker and we live on a horse farm in rural Pennsylvania where I am an active part of the homeschooling community.

I'm a proud member of the Women Empowerment Website Ring. Let's speak up and speak out about the things that are important to us!!

If you have something to say, send me a message online. I'd love to chat.

I CAN'T REMEMBER THE last time Mom and I had worked on a project together. Maybe it was when I was in the fourth grade and I had to do a poster for science and I started crying because the bar graphs weren't even. Mom got a level and a ruler from the garage and stayed up half the night with me until everything was perfect.

The night we read Dad's letter, we sat huddled together in our pajamas on the bed in Papa's guest room, the papers from the time capsule spread around us. Mom had a cup of coffee, determined, despite her jet lag, not to fall asleep until we had a plan.

Message to Amanda Vanderweele | Friday, July 17, 2015, 9:00 p.m.

9:01 PM

Anonymous (Claudia): Hi, this is Steve Dunlow, maybe you remember me from school? Anyway, I'm organizing our reunion and am trying to find an Amanda Vanderweele who went to George Washington Junior High. Any chance you're her?

9:08 PM

Amanda: Steve?! Of course I remember you!!!

Amanda: You were on the football team

Amanda: Remember the drive in?!

"Ewww, they made out!" I say.

"Give me the computer," Mom says.

9:09 PM

Anonymous (Mom): I sure do

Anonymous (Mom): How could I forget that?!

9:10 PM

Amanda: Giggle giggle

Amanda: It's great to hear from you

Anonymous (Mom): It's great to hear from you too!

Mom hands the computer back to me. "Just say what we planned, Claudia."

I start typing.

9:11 PM

Anonymous (Claudia): So listen. I'm trying to check all the addresses I have on file to make sure nobody misses an invite.

Amanda: You're sending paper?

Anonymous (Claudia): Yeah

Amanda: Very classy.

Anonymous (Claudia): Thanks. Anyway, I have you down as being in Reading, PA, but I can't read the street address.

Amanda: Oh, Crystal Holmes organized the reunion last time. And she always had the worst handwriting!

Anonymous (Claudia): So you live on . . . is it King Street?

Amanda: Ha! Not even close.

Amanda: It's 6784 Red Riding Court, Reading, PA. Zip is 19603

"And just like that, she gives a total stranger her address." I shake my head.

Mom smiles. "And I thought I needed to warn you about Internet safety."

9:13 PM

Anonymous (Claudia): Thanks! I'll make sure I put a "save-the-date" card in the mail tomorrow.

Amanda: Super. OMG, I'm so excited!

Amanda: It's so ironic, because I was actually just thinking about junior high! Do you remember Jeff Dalton?

I put the computer down. "She mentioned Dad!" I look at Mom. "What do we do?"

"Give it to me."

Anonymous (Mom): Not really

Amanda: Sure you do! Jeff. He broke his wrist at Jason's party in 7th grade

Anonymous (Mom): Oh yeah.

Amanda: Anyway, we've stayed in touch over the years, mainly just Christmas and birthdays. But he's been visiting me for the past couple of weeks. He's a teacher and doesn't work in the summer. My husband travels a lot and sometimes I get kinda lonely. It's been great to see him again.

Anonymous (Mom): Nice

Amanda: Do you need to confirm his address too? Cause I can go get him.

Anonymous (Mom): Oh no, his address is nice and clear.

Amanda: Cool. Well, I'll look forward to hearing from you again soon!

Anonymous (Mom): Bye!

Mom puts down the computer.

"We did it!" I say.

She nods.

"You're sneaky!"

Mom grins, but she's shaking like she was caught in a snowstorm and can't get warm.

"I can't believe it," she says. "We found your father."

Claudia Dalton's Cell Phone | Friday, July 17, 2015, 9:40 p.m.

Kate: What?! You found him?

Claudia: Yeah. Mom, Papa, and I are going to drive up and talk to him in the morning.

Kate: Does he know you're coming?

Claudia: No. Mom thought it would be better as a surprise. I think she's afraid he might try to run again.

Kate: Wow! Hope it goes well.

Claudia: Me too! How are you? Did your mom have the baby yet?

Kate: No.

Claudia: It's been like eight hours! How long does it take?!

Kate: We're still at the hospital. Her blood pressure is really high. She might need a C-section.

Claudia: Oh. Is she okay?

Kate: Yeah.

Claudia: Are you okay?

Kate: I think so. I'm just . . . a little worried. Women die during labor sometimes.

Claudia: Not often. Not if they're in the hospital.

Kate: I know, I know. It's just . . . I hate being here alone.

Claudia: You're not alone. Isn't your dad there?

Kate: Yeah, but I can't talk to him.

Claudia: Yes, you can.

Kate: Nah.

Claudia: I'm going to talk to mine.

Kate: Well, yours is a lot easier to talk to.

Claudia: Kate, he's two states away!

Kate: He cares about you. He spends time with you.

Claudia: Cares about me?! He ran away! Your dad is still there!

Kate: Claudia!

Claudia: I'm sorry. I shouldn't yell. I'm just worried too.

Kate: Of course you are. [SIGHS] Mom's sleeping now. They just gave her an epidural. Said it will still be a while. I guess I could ask my dad to get a snack in the cafeteria.

Claudia: Yes!

Kate: I don't know what to say to him.

Claudia: Me either. Guess we'll just have to hope we figure it out.

Kate: You were right about one thing.

Claudia: What's that?

Kate: I'm glad I'm here. Instead of sitting at home alone.

Claudia: That was all Luis, not me.

Kate: Hmm. This Luis. He's a smart guy?

Claudia: Yes, he is.

Kate: Well, I hope to meet him someday. He sounds like he's become a good friend.

Claudia: He has. Not better than you, but . . .

Kate: "There's enough love to go around." That's what my mom keeps saying.

Claudia: [LAUGHING] Maybe it's true.

Kate: We'll see.

Claudia: I better go. Good luck!

Kate: You too.

From: Holiday Inn <do-not-reply@holidayinn.com>

Date: Friday, July 17, 2015 9:43 PM EST

To: Jennifer Dalton <jennydalton431@gmail.com>

Subject: Holiday Inn Reservation, Reading, PA

Online Reservation:

Guest Name: Jennifer Dalton

Number of Adults: 2

Number of Children: 1

Room(s) Booked: 1

Room Type: Two Queen Beds, NONSM, Breakfast included

Check in: 3:00 PM 7/18/15

Check out: 12:00 NOON 7/19/15

We look forward to your visit!

From: Jenny Dalton <jennydalton431@gmail.com>
Date: Friday, July 17, 2015 9:55 PM EST
To: Julie Beckett <juliebeckett891@gmail.com>
Subject: Clear my schedule

Hi Julie,

Please clear my schedule for next week. I'm not going to be returning to the office on Monday as planned. I'm taking a few days off to deal with a personal matter.

Please send any urgent concerns to this email. Thanks.

Jenny

Claudia Dalton's Cell Phone | Friday, July 17, 2015, 10:07 p.m.

Luis: When do you leave?

Claudia: In the morning.

Luis: Wish I could come.

Claudia: Me too.

Luis: Take my camera.

Claudia: What?

Luis: You might want to record something.

Claudia: No, it's okay. If I want, I can just tape stuff on my phone.

Luis: Let's be honest, Claudia, the audio quality on your phone is horrible.

Claudia: Yeah, it is.

Luis: So you should take my camera.

Claudia: But . . .

Luis: I'll bring it back over now. With a few blank memory cards. And the tripod too. You know how to use it.

Claudia: But it's your most favorite possession!

Luis: But you're my most favorite friend.

Claudia: Thank you.

Luis: On my way.

YOUR TRIP TO:

Reading, PA

2 HR 59 MIN   165 miles

Driving time based on traffic as of 7:06 AM on July 18, 2015.

Current Traffic: Moderate

↑ Merge onto I-495N/Capital Beltway toward Baltimore

↗ Keep right to take I-95 N toward Baltimore

↑ Merge onto I-695 W via EXIT 49B on the left toward Towson

↑ Continue onto I-83 N

↱ Take exit 19 for PA-462/Market St

↑ Continue on US-222 N

↱ Exit onto US-422 E Penn St/Reading

INT. CAR—DAY

Papa is driving. Mom sits in the passenger seat. Claudia is filming from the back seat. It's a clear morning, the sun glinting off the river as they drive over a bridge.

For a long moment, no one says a word. Finally, Claudia clears her throat.

> CLAUDIA (O.S.)
> So, Mom, what do you think? About Dad . . .

> MOM
> Are we taking a poll? Raise your hand if you believe he's . . .

> CLAUDIA (O.S.)
> No. I just thought we could . . . never mind.

They lapse back into silence, but Claudia doesn't turn the camera off. Papa glances up into the rearview mirror, and the camera catches a glimpse of his eyes as he looks at his granddaughter. Mom sighs.

> MOM
> I'm sorry, Claudia. I don't mean to be snippy. I don't know what I think. My thoughts are so jumbled. All those years—why did I just keep waiting and hoping things would get better?

> PAPA
> It's good to be patient.

> MOM
> To a point. But then you just turn into an ostrich with your head in the sand. Where's the line?

                         CLAUDIA (O.S.)
Were things that bad?

                         MOM
I don't know. I mean, I was lonely, I knew something
was wrong, but I just ignored it. I didn't ask questions
or change anything or . . .

                         PAPA
Ignoring problems is a perfectly legitimate way to
maintain a marriage!

Mom tries to laugh.

                         PAPA (CONT'D)
This is not your fault, Jenny.

                         MOM
Whose is it, then?

Papa shrugs.

                         PAPA
No one's. Jeff's. Or maybe mine.

                         MOM
Yours? Why would it be your fault?

He changes lanes before answering.

                         PAPA
Do you remember that church Lily and I used to go to?
The one you and Jeff didn't want to get married in?

Yes.

                    PAPA

Ever since . . . I read the letter, I keep thinking about
some of the things our old pastor used to say. Horrible
things.

                    CLAUDIA (O.S.)

Like what?

                    PAPA

Like AIDS was God's punishment for homosexuals.

                    CLAUDIA (O.S.)

Did your pastor really say that?

                    PAPA

Yes, he did. In the 1980s, people said worse. I didn't
agree, even at the time, but I didn't say anything. I
didn't speak up. And so Jeff probably thought I agreed
with him.

                    MOM

It's not your fault either, Walter.

                    PAPA

Isn't it?

He drives in silence.

                    PAPA (CONT'D)

I want to hate that pastor for all those horrible things

he said. But when Lily was ill, he and his wife checked
in on us. Every single week. They'd call. Or drop by
groceries. Or send a card.

He shakes his head.

                              PAPA (CONT'D)
            And now I feel bad about that. Like I was betraying
            my son by accepting their help.

Mom pats him gently on the shoulder. Claudia sighs.

                              CLAUDIA (O.S.)
            When Dad first left, I blamed myself too. But now . . . I
            mean, I don't think people choose to be gay.

                              MOM
            I don't think so either.

They drive for a minute.

                              CLAUDIA (O.S.)
            So, do you think Dad is?

                              MOM
            That is a question for your father.

I JUST REALIZED ANOTHER reason I like taping conversations: The camera makes people feel brave. Like it's really important. Like they should risk asking and answering the hard questions, because the tape is rolling and it really counts.

I tried to hold on to that feeling as we drove up to Amanda's house.

EXT. AMANDA'S HOUSE—DAY

It's a nice country house, white, two stories, with a big front porch. Papa checks the address on the mailbox.

> PAPA
>
> This is it.

> MOM
>
> Okay. Come on.

The car doors slam and the picture wobbles as Claudia gets out of the car. Mom and Papa walk slowly toward the front porch.

There are big slate pavers leading to the steps. A well-manicured lawn. Two wooden rocking chairs on the sunny front porch. A pitcher of tea sits on a ledge, the sun shining bright through the mint, tea bags, and water.

Mom walks up to the front door and knocks. After only a moment, Amanda answers the door.

Amanda's blond hair is just beginning to thin and streak with gray. She's got an apron over her jeans and T-shirt and a baby balanced on her hip. She smiles extra big when she sees Mom.

> AMANDA
>
> Hello. What can I do for you?

> MOM
>
> Hi. Are you Amanda Vanderweele-Blume?

> AMANDA
>
> Yes, I am.

                              MOM

        This is a little awkward. You don't know me, but I'm
        looking for Jeff Dalton.

Amanda turns and calls into the house.

                            AMANDA

        Jeff! You have visitors.

She looks back at Mom and smiles again.

                        AMANDA (CONT'D)

        How do you know Jeff?

                              MOM

        I'm his wife.

Amanda laughs.

                            AMANDA

        Sweetie, I think you must have the wrong Jeff. 'Cause
        this one is gay.

Mom turns pale. She opens her mouth, but nothing comes out.

                             PAPA

        Is that what he told you?

Amanda glances at him. For the first time, she seems to realize
that something is odd about the situation.

                    AMANDA
        Do I know you, sir? You look kind of familiar. And
        why does that girl have a video camera?

A door slams inside the house. The stairs creak as someone walks
down them.

                    DAD (O.S.)
        I wasn't expecting . . .

Dad comes to the door. He's grown a short beard and wears biking
shorts and a T-shirt. He stares at the three of us, eyes wide, as if
we were ghosts. When the blood drains from his face, he looks like
the boy from the video, after the Death Star blew up.
    No one speaks.

                    CLAUDIA (O.S.)
        Hello, Dad.

                    AMANDA
        Have you been lying to me?!

                    MOM
        Claudia, turn off the camera.

The screen goes black.

AND THEN THERE are some things you shouldn't film, cause they're just too personal or upsetting or whatever. I remembered how I felt when I was reading the letter and I asked Luis to turn off the camera. So when Mom asked, I hit the off button.

But I can tell you about it, and I gotta say, seeing my father again wasn't exactly like I had imagined. He did give me a hug, an awkward, one-armed thing, but then Amanda started freaking out about how Dad had been lying to her. Mom just stood there calmly, but I felt a little glad that *someone* was yelling at him.

Then Amanda's baby started to cry and her other four kids ran out, and finally, we decided that she would take the kids to the park, Mom and Dad would sit on the front porch to talk, and Papa and I would go to a local coffee shop to wait until they were done.

Maple Hill
— CAFÉ —

134 Washington Street
Reading, PA 19601
7/18/15

Iced Mocha (extra whipped cream)	3.00
Coffee	3.00
Carrot Cupcake	3.00
Apple Pie	3.00
Subtotal:	12.00
Tax:	0.72
Total:	12.72

————————————————

INT. COFFEE SHOP—DAY

Papa and Claudia sit in a booth by a window. The shop isn't very crowded. They each have a cup and a plate with a treat in front of them.

                    CLAUDIA
        It isn't fair that Mom gets to talk to him first! I mean,
        he's your son. And I'm the one who did all those
        puzzles!

Papa smiles.

                    PAPA
        Yeah, well, there's not exactly an etiquette manual
        for this sort of thing.

                    CLAUDIA
        Guess not.

She takes a sip of her iced mocha.

                    PAPA
        How's your cupcake?

                    CLAUDIA
        Kinda dry. How's the pie?

                    PAPA
        It's okay. Listen, um, you're probably going home
        after this trip, but I just wanted to say, I'm really glad
        you came to stay with me this summer.

CLAUDIA

Me too.

PAPA

Watching all those home movies with you, well, it
made me realize I wasn't really the father I wanted to
be with Jeff. And with you here this summer, and us
working together on that treasure hunt, it's like I got
a second chance with you.

Claudia smiles.

CLAUDIA

Oh, Papa, that's so nice!

He reaches out and pats her hand, then looks away, embarrassed.

PAPA

This pie could really use a scoop of ice cream.

CLAUDIA

Everything's better with ice cream.

PAPA

That was my one parenting trick. If things are going
badly, buy the kid a snack.

CLAUDIA

Works for me! Remember those Popsicles we had
before the merry-go-round?

PAPA

I think my fingers are still sticky.

Claudia laughs.

                              CLAUDIA
          I don't think you did such a bad job, Papa. At least you
          didn't with me.

                              PAPA
          Thanks.

They smile shyly at each other. Then Papa pulls out his phone.

                              PAPA (CONT'D)
          I gotta call the hotel. Make sure they don't give away
          our room.

WHILE PAPA CALLED the hotel, I wandered over to the back of the shop, where there was a big table and a basket full of jigsaw puzzle pieces. Those puzzle pieces looked better to me than all the cupcakes in the display window. Finally, something familiar that I knew how to handle.

I dumped out the basket and started sorting. After a few minutes, I figured out there were three or four different puzzles, all jumbled up together. They were kid puzzles, none of them more than one hundred pieces, so they weren't too hard to put together, even without boxes to tell me the pictures.

One puzzle had a picture of puppies dressed like clowns. (Why? Who knows.) There were about three pieces missing from that one.

The next was a farm scene, and someone had chewed on all the pieces of the animals' heads. So strange. That one was missing five or six pieces. My bet was that some kid had eaten them.

Then there were a bunch of random pieces from some weird puzzle that I imagined must have been called "Zebras and Candy Canes." I'd never seen so many crazy stripes. There weren't enough pieces of that one to bother working it.

And finally, there was one more puzzle, probably about a hundred pieces. When I was done with that one, I saw a jungle scene, kinda like the one we had done with Nana before she died. A leopard family, a monkey, a parrot. Somehow, there were no pieces missing. I traced each piece slowly with my fingertips, wishing I could go back to the day before Dad had disappeared.

My phone beeped and I saw a text from Mom.

We're done talking. Dad says he's tired and he'll speak to you and Papa tomorrow. Come pick me up.

I couldn't text her back. I couldn't move. Dad was tired?! I was tired. And angry. And frustrated. Mom was right. I didn't want to be patient anymore. I wanted answers. Now! Or I wanted to put all the pieces back into the box and start again. Pick out a different puzzle. A different story. A different family. But I couldn't. There wasn't even a box. This was the puzzle I had gotten.

Then I had an idea.

I went to the barista and offered her five dollars for the pieces, but she said, "Just take whatever you want, no one ever works the puzzles anyway." I went back to my table, flipped the jungle puzzle over, pulled out a Sharpie from my purse, and wrote a message on the back. The nice barista gave me a plastic Ziploc bag, and I broke up the pieces and put them inside. Then I wrote on the outside of the bag: *To Dad.*

Claudia Dalton's Cell Phone | Tuesday, July 21, 2015, 5:23 p.m.

PHONE TRANSCRIPT

Claudia: And we drove back and picked Mom up. Since Dad was too "tired" to talk, I handed him the plastic bag.

Luis: And?

Claudia: And I'm sitting in the hotel game room now. There's a sad-looking foosball table and a couple of board games.

Luis: Did you tell your dad there was a message on the back of the puzzle?

Claudia: Nah. He can figure that out himself.

Luis: Yeah.

Claudia: I mean, duh, it's a message, right? That's how we communicate in my family—by jigsaw puzzle.

Luis: [LAUGHING] Some people use sign language . . .

Claudia: Some people speak French . . .

Luis: But you guys . . .

Claudia: It's tabs and pockets all the way.

Luis: Yup.

Claudia: He's pretty much an idiot if he can't figure that out.

Dad: [MUFFLED] I am an idiot.

Luis: Who's that?

Dad: [MUFFLED] Your mother said I might find you down here.

Claudia: [TO LUIS] I have to go.

Dear Dad,

Are you gay? Why did you run away instead
of telling me? Why didn't you think I would
understand?!
Please talk to me.

Love, Claudia

INT. HOTEL GAME ROOM—DAY

Claudia and her father sit across from each other, interview style. The bag of puzzle pieces rests on the table between them.

> DAD
>
> Do you have to tape this?

> CLAUDIA
>
> Yes.

> DAD
>
> I'd rather you didn't.

> CLAUDIA
>
> I'd rather you hadn't disappeared.

> DAD
>
> Fair enough.

Dad stretches. He's trying to stay calm, but his hands are shaking.

> DAD (CONT'D)
>
> What do you want to know?

> CLAUDIA
>
> Are you gay?

> DAD
>
> Not going to ease into this with a little small talk?

> CLAUDIA
>
> No. Are you gay?

                              DAD

        Yes.

                              CLAUDIA

        Can you say it?

                              DAD

        What do you want, Claudia?

                              CLAUDIA

        I want you to say it.

She crosses her arms.

                              DAD

        Sweetie, I want to talk to you, but I need you to—

Claudia stands up and slams her hands down on the table.

                              CLAUDIA

        I don't care about what you need! What about what *I*
        need?!

Dad sits there for a moment, staring at her. Finally, he takes a
deep breath.

                              DAD

        You're right. This conversation is for you. What do
        you need?

                              CLAUDIA

        Answers.

DAD

Okay. Then just sit back down and . . .

He gestures to the bag of puzzle pieces on the table.

DAD (CONT'D)

We can do the puzzle and I'll answer your questions.

Claudia thinks for a moment. Finally, she nods and sits back down. Dad dumps out the pieces and begins sorting.

Okay, so I hadn't realized I was so angry. I'd spent the past few weeks desperately trying to find him, wishing he would come back, thinking everything would be okay once he did.

I hadn't really thought about how hurt or scared I'd been. Until I saw him again. I knew I was acting like a jerk, but I just couldn't help it.

I needed a chance to think and calm down. Luckily, our conversation was saved—once again—by a puzzle.

INT. HOTEL GAME ROOM—CONTINUOUS

Dad works the edge pieces. Claudia puts together a jaguar family: mom, dad, baby. Neither of them speaks. Finally, Dad clears his throat.

                    DAD

        Yes, Claudia. I'm gay.

Claudia studies the pieces she's working on and asks her next question without looking at him.

                    CLAUDIA

        When did you know?

                    DAD

        I think I've always known. But I didn't want to accept
        it. I spent most of my teens trying to convince myself
        that everyone had same-sex feelings, but that they
        were just too personal to talk about.

                    CLAUDIA

        Did that work?

Dad shrugs.

                    DAD

        Not really.

                    CLAUDIA

        If you had those thoughts, why did you marry Mom?

                    DAD

        Because I loved her. She was my best friend. I thought

maybe getting married would make those feelings go
away.

CLAUDIA
That wasn't fair to Mom.

DAD
It wasn't. But, Claudia, when your mother and I were
dating, you couldn't be openly gay and be a teacher.
You couldn't get married. You couldn't have children.
I wanted all those things! And I saw no way to get
them as a gay man. So I decided to be straight.

CLAUDIA
You can't decide to be straight.

DAD
Of course you can't. No more than you can "decide"
to be gay. I know that now. But I didn't then.
I honestly thought if I worked hard enough,
if I prayed long enough, I could fix anything.
Including myself.

He works a few more pieces in silence.

DAD (CONT'D)
I thought I was broken. That there was something
wrong with me. It makes me so sad to think about
it now.

CLAUDIA
I still don't understand. If you realized those feelings
weren't going away, why didn't you just tell us?

DAD

I couldn't overcome the shame.

CLAUDIA

Shame about being gay?

DAD

No. I'd accepted that. About my dishonesty. I'd been
lying for years to those I loved the most. How could I
hurt you and Mom like that?

CLAUDIA

You hurt us by not telling us. You hurt us by running
away!

DAD

I know I did and I'm sorry. But when I saw those
happy couples on the news, celebrating their new
right to marry, well, I just couldn't go home and face
you and Mom. I wish I had done it differently, but I
thought I needed some time to . . . *try on* the decision
to come out.

CLAUDIA

What about that email you sent me? The one inviting
me to go with you to Papa's for the weekend? Were
you going to . . .

DAD

Yeah. I was thinking about telling you then.

CLAUDIA

I'm sorry I didn't say yes.

DAD

Claudia, this is not your fault. I'd been thinking about coming out for years. I thought maybe when you graduated high school, I . . . but then last February, when Nana died, I decided I didn't want to spend any more time pretending to be someone I wasn't. I had never given my mother a chance to know the real me; I didn't want to do that to you too.

CLAUDIA

But why the puzzles?

DAD

After the funeral, I realized many of the things I had done with Brian were things I had also done with you. So I found the first piece with C-3PO and put it in my wallet. I thought if you did the treasure hunt and watched the videos of when I was your age, maybe it would remind you of all the good times we've had together. Then maybe I could tell you the truth and you might still love me.

Claudia stops working the puzzle and looks up at him.

CLAUDIA

Of course I still love you, Dad!

Dad's eyes fill with tears, but he can't bring himself to speak.

CLAUDIA (CONT'D)

I'm mad as heck at you for leaving . . . but I still love you.

DAD

Good. Because I love you too. I know I did the wrong
thing, Claudia. I'm sorry I made a mess of coming
out. I wish I had been braver. I wish I had been a
fighter. I wish I had been like the others who fought
for the societal changes I couldn't even imagine. But
if I had, I wouldn't have had you. And being your
father . . . it wasn't all a lie, Claudia. I know it might feel
that way. But my love for you is not a lie.

Now Claudia's eyes fill with tears.

CLAUDIA

Are you coming home?

DAD

Yes. I bought a bus ticket back to Richmond for
tomorrow.

CLAUDIA

To our old house?

There are only a handful of pieces left now and they are working
them slowly, trying to make them last.

DAD

No. Mom and I talked about that. I'm going to get an
apartment.

CLAUDIA

You're going to get divorced?

                                    DAD
          I think so. But we'll always be a family, Claudia. And I
          will always love you.

Only three pieces left now.

                                  CLAUDIA
          I'll always love you too, Dad. But how do I know you
          won't leave again?

                                    DAD
          Because I won't.

                                  CLAUDIA
          But—

                                    DAD
          What I mean is, I know it's going to take a while for
          you to fully trust me again.

                                  CLAUDIA
          Yeah.

                                    DAD
          But that's okay. I can wait.

Claudia smiles. He hands her the last piece and she puts it into
place. They both stare at the completed puzzle, the happy animal
families smiling up at them.

                              DAD (CONT'D)
          Is there anything else you wanted to ask?

Claudia thinks for a moment.

                    CLAUDIA
        Yes. Actually, there is.

She gestures to his clothes.

                    CLAUDIA (CONT'D)
        What's with the outfit?

                    DAD
        What?

                    CLAUDIA
        I mean really, Dad. Biking shorts and a tight
        T-shirt?!

Dad smiles.

                    DAD
        Too much?

                    CLAUDIA
        You're a walking cliché.

He laughs.

                    DAD
        I was trying a new look!

                    CLAUDIA
        Remember that time I dyed my hair green?

                    DAD

     Yeah. It's that bad?

Claudia nods.

                  CLAUDIA

     Can't you just be gay in your dress shirts and math
     ties?

Dad laughs again.

                    DAD

     Are we okay, Claudia?

                  CLAUDIA

     Not yet. But I think we will be.

                    DAD

     Good.

And they both smile.

AND YEAH, SO I talked to my dad. And that's how it went. Not half bad, huh?

I was a little bit proud of myself. Before this summer, I probably would have run out right at the beginning, when all I could focus on was feeling mad. But I didn't this time. I thought about Luis saying he believed I could handle it, and Kate becoming a big sister when she was almost a teenager, and Mom feeling lonely, and Papa riding the merry-go-round, and Nana dying. Sometimes things change whether you want them to or not. So I stayed and I listened. And I'm glad I did.

Claudia Dalton's Cell Phone | Saturday, July 18, 2015, 7:19 p.m.

TEXT MESSAGE

KATE

He's here!!! Harrison James Anderson!!
We're calling him Harry
He's so cute!
Mom let me hold him
He smells good
I even changed a poopy diaper
Did you know it's not real poop at first?
OMG, I'm turning into a horrible baby crazy girl!!!

Haha. I'm so happy for you
The pic you sent was adorable
You're gonna be an awesome big sister

You think?

100% sure

You get to talk to your dad?

Yeah

And?

Gay

Huh

Tell you more when I get home

Okay
Guess what

What?

313

I talked to my dad too

You did?!
What happened?

I just blurted out that I was worried he
wouldn't have time for me once the baby came

And?

He apologized
Said he knew he had been working too much
Said he was worried too
Said I was amazing for taking that class
I'd have to give him pointers

Your dad made a joke?

Yeah

Do you think he'll really
stop working so much?

I don't know
I think he wants to
I think he cares
Maybe that's all I needed to hear

I'm glad you talked to him

Me too

How's your mom?

She's fine
Ended up with a C-section
But she's fine

I'm glad

How about your mom?

Hanging in there

And your dad?

He's coming home
Getting his own place
But coming home

And you?

Me?

How are you doing?

I don't know

Fair enough
Oh, I forgot to tell you!
My brother is wearing the
dinosaur outfit you sent him

Really?

Yeah
It's so sweet
Gotta go
Baby crying

See you soon!

Walter Dalton's Cell Phone | Saturday, July 18, 2015, 9:55 p.m.

[RECORDING BEGINS]

Lily, I just got a drink at the hotel bar with our son. Our gay son.

We didn't really say much, just sat at the bar and watched the baseball game. We mainly talked about Claudia and how great she is. There were all sorts of things I wanted to ask. But for now, it was enough just to sit and have a drink.

[RECORDING ENDS]

From: Jeffery Dalton <jeffdalton327@gmail.com>
Date: Sunday, July 19, 2015 10:55 AM EST
To: Claudia Dalton <claudiadalton195@gmail.com>
Subject: Thanks

Dear Claudia,

It was good to talk to you yesterday. I know it wasn't easy, but I wanted to say thank you. For watching the videos. For following the pieces. For digging up the letter. For coming to find me. And for pushing me to say it aloud. Because it felt different when I said it to you out loud, instead of just inside my head. It made me believe that even though things might not be okay right now, maybe they will be. Someday.

There are many things I wish I could do over. But having you as a daughter is not one of them. I love you.

Love, Dad

INT. CAR—DAY

Papa's behind the wheel again. Mom sits in the passenger seat. After a minute, Mom glances back at Claudia.

                    MOM
    You filming again?

                    CLAUDIA (O.S.)
    Yeah.

                    MOM
    Mmm.

                    CLAUDIA (O.S.)
    What are you thinking?

                    MOM
    Nothing.

                    CLAUDIA (O.S.)
    Come on. There's this little way you bite your lip when
    you're concentrating.

Mom smiles, but looks back out the window before she speaks.

                    MOM
    I was thinking about those postcards your father sent
    me when I was in France.

                    PAPA
    Postcards? Why?

                    MOM

        He put all these famous quotes on them. I'd always
        thought they were so sweet and romantic. But now,
        all I can think about is how he only used other
        people's words, and never his own.

                  CLAUDIA (O.S.)

        Are you angry?

                    MOM

        Angry?

She sounds surprised.

                  MOM (CONT'D)

        I think I will be angry. I should be angry, right? He
        lied to us for many years. But right now, I just feel
        relieved.

                   PAPA

        Relieved?

                    MOM

        Now I know I'm not crazy. Not imagining things. Now
        I know why. Why no matter how hard I tried, it never
        made a difference.

They all think about that for a long moment. Finally, Claudia's
phone buzzes.

                  CLAUDIA (O.S.)

        It's a text from Dad.

                    MOM
What'd he say?

                    CLAUDIA (O.S.)
He sent me the "mixtape"!

Claudia Dalton's Cell Phone | Sunday, July 19, 2015, 11:40 a.m.

 PLAYLIST

1980s Playlist

▶ PLAY   ⤭ SHUFFLE

1. The Power of Love
   Huey Lewis and the News

2. Addicted to Love
   Robert Palmer

3. If You Love Somebody Set Them Free
   Sting

4. Faith
   George Michael

5. Papa Don't Preach
   Madonna

6. I Just Can't Stop Loving You
   Michael Jackson

7. Livin' on a Prayer
   Bon Jovi

8. I Just Called to Say I Love You
   Stevie Wonder

9. What's Love Got to Do with It
   Tina Turner

10. The Greatest Love of All
    Whitney Houston

Claudia Dalton's Cell Phone | Sunday, July 19, 2015, 10:45 p.m.

Luis: You still up?

Claudia: Yeah. You okay?

Luis: That was . . . some intense footage.

Claudia: Yeah. Maybe I shouldn't have shown it to you.

Luis: No, I was glad you wanted me to see it. I just couldn't find the words I wanted once it was done.

Claudia: That's okay.

Luis: It's easier now. On the phone. When I don't have to look at you. [PAUSE] That sounded stupid. I like looking at you. But . . .

Claudia: No, I get it. I think my dad felt the same way. It's like he couldn't really talk to me until we had something else to do.

Luis: Until you started the puzzle.

Claudia: Yeah.

Luis: Yeah. It's funny, last summer, my mom and I did nothing but argue. But then, when she was driving me back to my dad's, we had the best conversation.

Claudia: Thank you for loaning me your camera.

Luis: Thanks for trusting me with your story.

Claudia: That's what friends do.

Luis: Yeah. It is.

MOM AND I decided to stay with Papa for a few more days. We wanted to give Dad time to get home and move out. He found an apartment, a two-bedroom, and bought a bunch of stuff from IKEA to fill it up. It was strange how fast things were changing. Only a month before, we'd been at home, celebrating Dad's birthday.

I spent a lot of time thinking: If I stumbled across a Time-Turner or a TARDIS, would I go back in time and change things? (Okay, so Luis and I had probably been watching too much *Harry Potter* and *Doctor Who*.)

Forget the obvious for a moment—if Mom and Dad hadn't gotten married, I wouldn't be here—and let's just assume, for the sake of the argument, that I was. Which of all my memories would I be willing to give up?

Building the space station with Dad? Reading at the pool? Learning to work a puzzle? And those are just the old memories. What about going on the merry-go-round with Papa? Or learning to work a video camera with Luis? Or scheming over text messages with my mom? I don't want to give up any of them!

And so I decided I'd just have to get used to the pieces I've been given, even if they don't form the picture I had imagined they would.

Anyway, that's what I was thinking while I walked through the aisles at the grocery store with Papa. He was planning another cookout so I could say good-bye to Luis and his family. Papa paused in the meat aisle. "Hot dogs?" he asked. "They were Nana's favorite," I said. And he put them in the cart.

GIANT FOOD
425 E. Monroe Avenue
Alexandria, VA 22301
Store Telephone: (703) 555-8149

Store #752   7/24/15   11:15 AM

GROCERY

ALL BEEF HOT DOGS	3.99
TURKEY HOT DOGS	4.99
BALLPARK FRANKS	3.99
HOT DOG BUNS	1.99
CORN (on the cob)	
BONUS BUY SAVINGS	0.15-
PRICE YOU PAY	1.84

Total Before Savings	16.95
Your Savings	0.15
Total After Savings	16.80
TAX	0.42
**BALANCE	17.22

****

Payment Type: CREDIT
Card: **** **** **** 6342
Payment Amt: $ 17.22

EXT. PAPA'S BACKYARD—NIGHT

Claudia stands on a chair, hanging lights on a big umbrella. Papa is at the gas grill, cooking the hot dogs. Stewart follows Mariana as she totters around the patio. She keeps pulling petals off flowers and squealing in delight. Luis's mom and Claudia's mom sit at the picnic table, each drinking a glass of wine.

> MRS. FERNANDEZ
> Well, I have a friend I could recommend.

> MOM
> Really?

> MRS. FERNANDEZ
> Sure.

> MOM
> Oh, that'd be great.

> MRS. FERNANDEZ
> She's technically a mediator.

Stewart calls out from the flower bed.

> STEWART
> So much cheaper if you can do it that way!

> MRS. FERNANDEZ
> Then you consult with a lawyer to look over the
> agreement. Make sure everything is fair.

She hands Mom her card.

                              MOM

      Thank you.

Mrs. Fernandez squeezes her hand.

                        MRS. FERNANDEZ

      You're going to be okay.

Claudia jumps down from the chair and looks over at Papa.

                            CLAUDIA

      Dinner ready yet?

                              PAPA

      Few more minutes.

Claudia nods and walks over to a card table. She picks up a box
and turns to the camera.

                            CLAUDIA

      Luis, one last puzzle?

                           LUIS (O.S.)

      Sure.

                              MOM

      Which one are you doing?

Claudia holds up the box for the camera.

                            CLAUDIA

      It's "River in the Jungle."

PAPA

That's the last one we did with Lily, isn't it?

CLAUDIA

Yeah, it is.

No one says anything for a minute.

PAPA

Hot dogs and puzzles—almost like she's here.

He smiles.

LUIS (O.S.)

Go on, then! Dump it out.

Claudia opens the box and pours the pieces all over the table. They fall everywhere, each different and colorful, each with tabs and pockets, each telling its own separate bit of the story.

And nestled under the pieces, shining bright on the dark card table, is a white envelope.

Slowly, Claudia pulls it out of the pile and shakes off the pieces. Luis zooms in.

In Nana's delicate handwriting are the words *To my dear son, Jeff.*

Claudia Dalton's Cell Phone | Friday, July 24, 2015, 5:45 p.m.

Claudia: Dad?

Dad: Hi, Claudia. What's up?

Claudia: We were doing this puzzle. The jungle one, the last one we did with Nana. And we found an envelope in the box. From Nana. I think it's a letter to you!

Dad: What?!

Claudia: Do you want us to send it to you or . . .

Dad: I can't wait! Open it right now and read it to me.

Claudia: Are you sure?

Dad: Absolutely.

L M D

January 23, 2015

Dearest Jeff,

   I have a confession to make. Maybe I'm not quite on my deathbed, but close enough.

   Long ago, that year when you were friends with Brian, I thought you might be a homosexual. The thought made me very angry and afraid. I never spoke a word about it to you. You had that friend Amanda for years. And I always thought maybe the two of you would . . . but it never happened. Years later, when you brought Jenny home and introduced her as your girlfriend, I rejoiced, and not just because Jenny is a lovely person, but because it meant my suspicions were wrong.

   Unless they weren't. I've had lots of time to think during chemo. I used to believe finding out my son was gay would be the worst thing in the world. But although I am so proud of you and all you have accomplished, you don't seem very happy. I've spent a lot of time wondering why. The world has changed. Guess I've changed too. Because now I think that the

329

L M D

worst thing of all would not be finding out my son was gay, but finding out he felt like he had to pretend to be something he wasn't, not just as a child, but for his whole life.

I don't want that for you, Jeff.

Perhaps I am wrong. Perhaps this is just the drug-induced musing of a dying woman. If I am wrong, please forgive me. But if I'm not, please know, dearest Jeff, that I love you no matter what. And if my suspicions are true, please be patient with your father. It might take time for him to come around, but he loves you so very much.

I'm sorry I'm not brave enough to speak with you about this in person, but trying to survive another month, another week, another day is taking all my strength. I hope you will forgive me for all my failings. You were a wonderful son!

Love,
Mom

S O YEAH, YEAH, everyone cried over the note from Nana. Then we laughed over how similar she and Dad were, only daring to say what they had to say in notes, and then hiding them away.

Papa forgot the hot dogs and burned them for real, not just a little, but we ate them anyway and they were delicious. After dinner, I took a photo of the letter and texted it to Dad. He called back when he'd read it over again and he and Papa talked for a long time.

When Papa hung up, he looked happier than he had in months, really, happier than he had been since Nana had died.

EXT. PAPA'S BACKYARD—NIGHT

Mom sits alone at the picnic table. She doesn't look happy. Claudia sits down beside her. They stare at the lights on the umbrella.

                    MOM
        I guess everyone knew except for me.

Claudia says nothing, just puts her head on Mom's shoulder. A moment later, Mrs. Fernandez comes outside and sits down on the other side of the table.

                    MRS. FERNANDEZ
        You okay, Jenny?

Mom shakes her head.

                    MOM
        I feel like such a fool!

                    MRS. FERNANDEZ
        I suspect this is going to feel pretty awful for a while.

Mom nods but doesn't speak.

                    MRS. FERNANDEZ (CONT'D)
        You know, when I got divorced, people called me a fool
        too. "What did you expect?!" they said. "If you marry
        a dreamer, of course you're going to argue about
        money!" I felt so stupid. Like I had done something
        wrong. Until I realized, when people blame you for
        what's happened, they aren't really talking about you
        at all. They're trying to reassure themselves that
        nothing bad will happen to them.

MOM

Yeah. Maybe so.

MRS. FERNANDEZ

And when they do that, they miss the point. Because the best part of having something bad happen is learning you have the strength to pick up the pieces and keep going.

Mom's lips quiver and her eyes get very wide.

MRS. FERNANDEZ (CONT'D)

Oh, go ahead and cry. None of us mind.

So Mom does.

I T'S STRANGE, BUT watching Mom cry actually made me feel a little better. It was the first time I'd seen her not try to be strong for me, and it was sort of a relief. Like I could break down once in a while too, and I'd still be okay.

Eventually, Mom stopped crying and we all went and worked on the jigsaw puzzle. I had to show Papa how to sort the edge pieces, and told Mom to work on the red pieces, and Luis's little sister tried to eat a couple of them, but finally we finished.

Then we had ice cream cones, and Mariana fell down and started screaming, and Stewart took her home to put her to bed while Papa cleaned the grill and the moms tidied up.

And Luis and I, well, we sat on the front porch and looked at the stars.

At least we tried to look at the stars. But this close to the city, there was too much light pollution, so we watched the airplanes instead. I thought about all the people in all those planes. And all their stories. About how some were happy and some were sad and most were both. I thought about how sometimes you could buy your plane ticket and be super organized and early to the airport and everything, and still something could happen. There could be a thunderstorm or a fuel pipe could spring a leak or a pilot could get a flat tire on the way to the airport.

And then you had a choice. You could get mad and cry and pout and let it ruin your trip. Or you could shrug and readjust. You could go back to the gelato shop and try a new flavor. Buy a magazine at the overpriced store. Or even just sit and talk to a few of the other people who were stuck there with you.

I turned to say something to Luis and found he was already looking at me. No, he was staring at me. It was kinda weird.

"What?" I asked.

"Nothing." He glanced away, then back at me again.

"What?!" I asked, blushing. "What are you doing?"

"Truthfully?" he said. "The Jedi mind trick."

And then I stopped thinking about the planes.

"Really?" I asked. "On me?"

"Yup."

"Oh." He looked so cute in the streetlight. His hair all out of place. Some ketchup on his cheek.

"It's not working," he sighed.

"Are you sure about that?"

He didn't say anything. But I gazed at him. And then he leaned forward and then I leaned forward, and then suddenly we were kissing.

And I felt hot and cold, then hot again. And my skin tingled and my heart pounded and I felt dizzy.

"Oh!" I said breathlessly.

And Luis smiled.

Walter Dalton's Cell Phone | Saturday, July 25, 2015, 9:15 a.m.

[RECORDING BEGINS]

Papa: Hi, Lily. Claudia is here with me today. She wanted to say a little something before she goes home.

Claudia: Hi, Nana! I can't believe Papa kept it a secret this whole time that he was talking to you like this. 'Cause I totally would have wanted to talk to you too.

Papa: Well, sorry!

Claudia: I just wanted to say we're doing all right. We found Dad. Mom's okay. And Papa did all this cool stuff with me this summer.

Papa: We went to a bunch of those museums you were always trying to get me to go to.

Claudia: And guess what, Nana? He liked them!

Papa: I did not!

Claudia: Yes, you did.

Papa: Well, maybe a little.

Claudia: We had a good summer, didn't we, Papa?

Papa: We certainly did.

Claudia: Love you, Nana!

[RECORDING ENDS]

WHEN I WENT over to say good-bye to Luis, his mother came to the door. I thanked her for being so kind to my mother. She smiled, of course, and said it was nothing. But then, as she went to call Luis, I thought of one more thing I needed to say.

"You really should watch his movie!"

Mrs. Fernandez turned back to look at me. In her fancy church dress, with her black hair slicked back into a neat bun, she looked intimidating. How could I tell her what to do? And yet I owed it to Luis to try.

"I mean, I haven't seen it yet, no one has, but . . . he's good at talking to people. And listening to them and helping them share their stories. At least he was with me. And I know he's really smart and he'd be a great doctor, or lawyer, or engineer, but . . . I think he'd be pretty good at documentaries too."

She laughed then and took my hand. "You're right, Claudia." She smiled again, more warmly this time, and promised that she would.

Luis had copied all the videos he'd recorded onto a portable hard drive and packed it in a little red box so I could watch them whenever I wanted.

I don't know how his movie is going to turn out or what it's going to say about me and my family. I don't know what the story of this summer will look like from his point of view. But I told him about my plans to make this binder and said he could read it if he wanted when I was done.

We promised we'd stay in touch, and I think we will.

Claudia Dalton's Cell Phone | Saturday, July 25, 2015, 1:45 p.m.

KATE

Home

Yay!!
Come over and meet little Harry?

On my way

LEASE AGREEMENT

BASIC CONDITIONS _____

_____

_____

THE PARTIES IN THIS AGREEMENT ARE:

The "Landlord" (in this lease the term "Landlord" means either the owner or his agent) AND___*Jeffery Dalton*___ the "Tenant/s"

PREMISES TO BE RENTED

Address ___*175 West Elm St., Apt 3A, Richmond, VA*___

_____

TERM

The landlord hereby leases to the Tenant the premises described above for a term of ONE YEAR, from ___*August 1, 2015*___ to ___*July 31, 2016*___

RENT

The monthly rent is $___*1200*___.

The rent is payable on the ___*15*___th day of the month.

Rent payment shall be paid to: ___*Landlord*___ at the following address: ___*175 West Elm St., Apt 1A*___.

DAD HAS CALLED every day since we talked in the hotel game room. Sometimes we say a lot, and sometimes we just chat about the weather. If he's running late to pick me up, even just by five minutes, he always texts or calls. "I don't want you to worry . . ." Dad says.

And he's trying so hard I usually don't.

From: Brian Tuckerman <briantuckerman17@gmail.com>

Date: Wednesday, March 7, 2012 7:45 PM EST

To: Jeffery Dalton <jeffdalton327@gmail.com>

Subject: Hello from an Old Friend

Hi Jeff,

It's been forever, hasn't it? My 20th high school reunion is coming up soon and I've been feeling a little nostalgic. So I started looking up a bunch of people I used to know in school. I found your email online. A teacher, huh? Bet you're a great one.

I'm a lawyer now, and way too busy, but it pays the bills. My wife and kids complain that they'd like to see me more, but I do the best I can. I'd love to hear what you've been up to. If you ever want to chat, reply to this email or give me a call sometime. 301-555-9874

I'm sorry we ended . . . on odd terms. I've always wondered what happened to you and wished we had stayed in touch. Anyway, hope all is well!

Best, Brian

— — — — — — — — — — — —

From: Jeffery Dalton <jeffdalton327@gmail.com>

Date: Monday, August 17, 2015 9:31 AM EST

To: Brian Tuckerman <briantuckerman17@gmail.com>

Subject: Re: Hello from an Old Friend

Hi Brian,

I'm sorry it took me three years to respond to your email! I've started and restarted this message about a million times. I'm sorry for the way I ended our friendship all those years ago. It's been a bit of a rough year. I recently came out to my wife and daughter and I'm getting divorced.

So, if you would still be willing to chat, it would mean a lot.

Best, Jeff

——————————————

From: Brian Tuckerman <briantuckerman17@gmail.com>
Date: Monday, August 17, 2015 10:23 AM EST
To: Jeffery Dalton <jeffdalton327@gmail.com>
Subject: Re: Hello from an Old Friend

Sure, buddy! Give me a call :)

INT. KITCHEN—NIGHT

Mom and Claudia are at the sink in the kitchen, side by side, washing dishes.

> **MOM**
>
> A game, huh?

> **CLAUDIA**
>
> Yep.

> **MOM**
>
> Where you get to ask a question and then I get to ask
> a question?

> **CLAUDIA**
>
> Yup. Think of it as truth or dare, but without the
> dares.

Mom laughs.

> **MOM**
>
> Sure, why not?

> **CLAUDIA**
>
> Great, I'll go first.

She scrubs a glass carefully while she thinks.

> **CLAUDIA (CONT'D)**
>
> Aren't you mad?

> **MOM**
>
> With who?

                         CLAUDIA

        Dad. He lied to you for years and years. How can you
        be okay with that?

                         MOM

        I'm not okay with that. But my anger isn't your
        problem, Claudia. I want you to be free to love us
        both.

                         CLAUDIA

        Did you know? Did you have any clue?

                         MOM

        I thought we each got one question.

                         CLAUDIA

        Oh yeah, sorry.

                         MOM

        It's okay. That question's just kind of embarrassing.

                         CLAUDIA

        That's the point of truth or dare.

Mom smiles.

                         MOM

        I didn't know. In retrospect, sure, there were signs.
        Your father never even looked at other women. I
        thought I had the most sensitive and polite husband
        ever.

She shrugs.

                    MOM (CONT'D)
I see it differently now.

                    CLAUDIA
It's not your fault, Mom.

                    MOM
I know. And it's not your job to worry about me.

She gives Claudia a quick, sudsy hug.

                    MOM (CONT'D)
So it's my turn now?

                    CLAUDIA
Yep.

                    MOM
Any question I want?

                    CLAUDIA
Go for it.

                    MOM
What's the hardest part of all this for you?

Claudia scrubs at an already clean plate.

                    CLAUDIA
How surprising it all was. I always thought we had a
great family.

                    MOM

We do have a great family!

                  CLAUDIA

Yeah. But now it's . . . different.

                    MOM

Different doesn't have to be bad.

                  CLAUDIA

I know.

                    MOM

I'm sorry, Claudia. I know how difficult it must be for
you. Being twelve is hard enough without having to
think about your parents' sexuality.

                  CLAUDIA

Lalala! Not listening.

Mom laughs.

                    MOM

But you know, I think there was an underlying
tension and dissatisfaction in our family that I didn't
see until Dad moved out and it went away.

                  CLAUDIA

Yeah. You seem . . . happier now. More at ease.

                    MOM

I think I am.

They scrub in comfortable silence for a moment.

                    MOM (CONT'D)
          You know, if you ever *liked* someone—boy or girl—I'd
          want you to feel comfortable talking to me about it.

                    CLAUDIA
          Gosh, Mom, that would never be comfortable!

Mom smiles.

                    CLAUDIA (CONT'D)
          But I would.

                    MOM
          Good. Because I don't want you to ever feel as alone as
          your dad did.

                    CLAUDIA
          I'd talk to you, Mom. But . . . I'm pretty sure I'm not
          gay.

                    MOM
          Really?

Claudia blushes.

                    CLAUDIA
          Well, Luis kissed me before we came home. And I
          liked it.

Mom stops washing dishes.

                    MOM
     Really?!

                  CLAUDIA
     Embarrassing alert! Embarrassing alert!

Mom grins.

                    MOM
     He seems like a nice boy.

                  CLAUDIA
     Very nice. Let us never speak of him again.

Mom laughs and goes back to washing dishes.

                    MOM
     You know, something good has already come out of
     all this.

                  CLAUDIA
     What?

Mom studies her soapy sponge.

                    MOM
     We never talked like this before.

No, we didn't.

I like it.

Me too.

NEED TO ASK for a camera like Luis's for Christmas. Because the audio quality on my phone really *is* terrible.

But the quality of the conversations with my parents, well, that's gotten a whole lot better.

NOTE TO READER

Claudia Dalton's Cell Phone | Saturday, August 22, 2015, 4:55 p.m.

LUIS

Did you get out yet?

> Movie just finished

What'd you think?

> It was great!

I know!! Best Jurassic Park movie since the original

> Yup
> Chris Pratt is so cute!!

Haha
I like the red-haired girl myself
But who tries to run from a T-Rex in heels?!

> I know!
> I was yelling at the screen
> for her to take them off

Me too!

> This was fun, Luis
> Watching a movie in different states
> Texting before and after

Let's do it again
Inside Out next time?

> Sounds like a plan

EXT. DAD'S NEW APARTMENT—DAY

A nondescript door. Labeled 3A. A hand comes into the frame and knocks.

                    DAD (O.S.)

        Come in!

Claudia opens the door and walks inside.

INT. DAD'S NEW APARTMENT—CONTINUOUS

It's an older two-bedroom apartment, but large and sunny. There's a couch in one corner. It's the one that used to be in Papa's attic, next to the puzzles.

                    DAD

        Hi, sweetie!

He's setting the table for lunch on a round dinette table at the other end of the room. He still has the beard and is wearing a T-shirt, but has traded the shorts for jeans.

                    DAD (CONT'D)

        Do you like the place?!

                    CLAUDIA (O.S.)

        Very nice.

Dad turns around. His shirt has a picture of a triangle, a hippo, and the formula $a^2 + b^2 = c^2$. Dad points to his shirt.

                    DAD
          Look! The longest side of a triangle. Instead of
          "hypotenuse," it's "hippotenuse." Get it?!

Claudia laughs.

                    CLAUDIA (O.S.)
          Math humor. Yes, I like that look!

Dad grins.

                    DAD
          Your bedroom's off to the right.

                    ————

INT. CLAUDIA'S NEW BEDROOM—DAY
Claudia opens the door. On the bed are the old Charlie Brown
sheets. And on the wall behind is the *Star Wars* poster.

                    DAD
          You can get new sheets and posters, of course. Those
          are just so it wouldn't be totally empty.

                    CLAUDIA (O.S.)
          I like them!

                    DAD
          You do?

                    CLAUDIA (O.S.)
          Yeah. For now.

                    DAD

Good.

                    CLAUDIA (O.S.)
I brought you a housewarming gift.

                    DAD

You did?

Claudia fumbles in her overnight bag and pulls out a wrapped
box. The contents shift as she hands it to her father, the sound of
pieces being jostled.

                    DAD (CONT'D)
I think I know what this is.

He grins and rips the paper off. It's a puzzle, of course. There's
a gay pride rainbow flag on the front. He can't speak for a
moment.

                    CLAUDIA (O.S.)
You like it?

                    DAD

I love it.

                    CLAUDIA (O.S.)
Did I see a coffee table in the living room?

                    DAD

Yes.

                    CLAUDIA (O.S.)
Perfect for a puzzle.

                         DAD
Well, then. Let's get started.

AND SO WE did. We all got started on our new lives. Mom filed for divorce and Dad started being honest about who he was and I got used to two houses. (It wasn't as bad as I expected.) And Kate learned to be a big sister, and Luis edited his movie, and I started seventh grade.

Dad and I don't hang upside down on the monkey bars anymore, but we still work puzzles, when I'm not hanging out with my friends. I asked him to start putting notes in my lunch again too—who cares what Billy Peterson thinks! I guess I see Dad more now, not as the perfect father who was always so much fun, but as a person. I understand that he sometimes screws up, often does okay, and always does the best he can.

Occasionally, I hear Mom crying in the shower. I pretend not to notice, not because I don't care, but because I understand why she's upset. Sometimes I feel like I should be mad at him for her, but like she always says, that's her problem, not mine, and I can love them both. Mom's dyed her hair and got new glasses and took up salsa dancing, which is SUPER embarrassing . . . and kinda cool too.

And get this . . . Papa was the first one to start dating! A real nice widow moved in with her daughter down the street. I don't know if Mom or Dad is dating yet—and I'm glad I don't know.

The three of us are going to drive up to Papa's for Thanksgiving and meet Papa's new girlfriend. Luis and his family are coming too. It's gonna be a little awkward, and Mom keeps telling me it's just for this one year. We probably won't do it next year. But that's okay. This year we are.

And me? I made this binder because I needed to figure things out. Needed to understand how my family could be both great and broken, all at the same time. Needed to tell my own story.

As I said in the beginning, I used to think that life was like a puzzle. And if I worked hard enough, it would look just like it did on the box. But I don't believe that anymore. I still think life is like a puzzle, but there's no box. The only picture is in your head, and it might be wrong, might not be the puzzle you're actually doing at all.

Sometimes, pieces from different puzzles get mixed together, and no matter how hard you try, you can't get them to fit. Even if you force a piece into place, eventually you realize your mistake, take it out, and go on. I guess that's what happened to Mom and Dad. Both good puzzles. Both good stories. For a while, they thought they went together, and now they don't.

But that's okay. I realized something else when I was doing all those puzzles this past summer. We don't do puzzles to see the picture. The fun of puzzles is in the pieces, putting them in and taking them out, trying new ones, and finally figuring out where the old ones go. It's celebrating getting all the red pieces together and not getting too upset that all the green ones are still a jumbled mess. It's completing the frame, and then having someone accidentally swipe it onto the floor and having to start all over again.

I used to think that happiness was knowing where all the pieces went. Having them all laid out in perfect order. But now I think I just might be wrong about that. Maybe the joy in life is in the jumble.

At least that's my theory. Your story might be a different one. I say grab a binder. If you want, I've got some extra notebook tabs to share.

Claudia Dalton
November 2015

AUTHOR'S NOTE

WHILE *THE JIGSAW JUNGLE* is a work of fiction, it was, like my other books, inspired by actual events. In August 2012, my husband of thirteen years acknowledged he was gay. He moved out a month later and our divorce was finalized in December 2013.

As embarrassed and traumatized as I was when this happened, I quickly realized I was not the only one to go through this experience. According to the Straight Spouse Network (SSN), an organization dedicated to supporting heterosexual spouses and partners of LGBTQ people, there are up to 2 million mixed-orientation couples. In 2017, the SSN averaged 173 support requests a month, coming from all fifty states. There's even a hit series on Netflix, *Grace and Frankie*, that has Jane Fonda and Lily Tomlin going through a similar predicament.

When a family changes, the task of creating a cohesive narrative of our lives—no matter what our sexual orientation—is difficult for everyone, but it seems especially hard on preteens/teens, who are just beginning to grapple with their own romantic feelings and sexuality. I wanted to write this book for them, for those kids who were caught up in a similar situation, so they might not feel so alone. As I wrote, I realized I was continuing a theme that shows up in all my books: that prejudice does not only hurt those being discriminated against. The fight to end injustice is important, not only because it is the right thing to do, but because it benefits us all.

As to my own story, six years later my kids are happy, healthy, do well in school, have friends, are sweet, kind, and loads of fun. In other words, they're absolutely fine. In many ways, we were lucky—my ex never abandoned us; he was (and remains) a caring, loving, and involved father; our social and financial support systems remained strong. Our family doesn't look like I imagined it would, the transition wasn't easy or without pain, but the journey to honesty in our family was definitely worth it.

Here's to a world where we can all be who we are!

Kristin Levine
Alexandria, Virginia
February 2018

RESOURCES:
STRAIGHT SPOUSE NETWORK: WWW.STRAIGHTSPOUSE.ORG
PFLAG: WWW.PFLAG.ORG

KEEP READING FOR MORE
FROM KRISTIN LEVINE

CHAPTER 1

I Have (Not So Much) Confidence

I T WAS JUST a metal detector. You know, the normal kind they have at airports to make sure no one smuggles a gun or a bomb or an iguana onto a flight. Millions of people go through them every day without a problem: old people, babies, pregnant women. But I couldn't shake the feeling that it was actually a cancer-causing death trap.

Come on! you're probably saying. *Everyone knows they're safe.*

But everyone used to think that X-ray machines at shoe stores were safe. My dad told me this story of how he took a bazillion photos of the bones in his foot one summer. And then that fall, his left baby toe got a wart, and he had to have surgery. Coincidence? I think not.

Okay, so maybe that's not the best example. In Dooms-day Journal #2, page 14, I have a section on how warts are caused by viruses caught by touching contaminated surfaces, such as a locker-room floor—or an X-ray machine used by every kid in town. And metal detectors don't use X-rays; they actually use non-ionizing radiation, but that's beside the point.

The point is, I wanted to go visit my father in Austria. He'd moved there four months earlier. I missed him. A lot. But if I wanted to see him, I had to walk through the metal detector.

Unfortunately, my brain overreacts sometimes. It tells me that many, many things are dangerous, and not things that lots of people think are scary, like making new friends or public speaking or math tests. I'm actually okay with all of those. No, *my* brain tells me I should avoid certain things that most people believe are safe. Like metal detectors.

Of course, logically I understood my fear didn't make much sense. But I still didn't want to walk through that beeping monstrosity. I could practically see the rays zapping each person who walked through, mutating harmless freckles into skin cancer. The line got shorter and shorter. I started gulping down air, trying to catch my breath.

"Are you all right, Becca?" my mom asked.

She was flying to Austria with me. Not to see my father—they'd been happily divorced for years—but so she could take a summer backpacking trip through Europe. I was glad she was traveling with me, but I was also a little embarrassed. I mean, I was twelve. I should have been able to get onto a plane by myself. All I had to do was sit there. My friend Chrissy started flying to Atlanta by herself each summer to see her grandparents when she was eight. But we all knew there was no way I'd be able to get on a plane alone.

Planes. Sometimes they crash and explode. No, I can't think about that now. I have to get through the metal detector first.

"Yes," I squeaked. "I'm fine."

Mom knew I was lying. She took my hand and squeezed it. It was clammy and cold. I tried to distract myself, like Dr. Teresa told me to do. Focus on Austria. Austria. *The Sound of Music.* Happy children frolicking in the Alps. *Doe, a deer, a female deer . . .* and . . . and . . .

Suddenly, we were at the front of the line. Mom moved smoothly and efficiently, like a cat, carefully putting her purse and backpack onto the conveyor belt. My joints felt stiff, my arms and legs suddenly too long, as I struggled to pull off my backpack and place it in the bin. I lumbered back to our spot in line, as if I were Pinocchio right after he came to life.

"Do you want to go first, sweetie?" Mom asked.

I shook my head.

"Come on, ma'am," the guard called. "Please step on through."

Mom squeezed my hand one last time and walked away. A moment later, she was through. My mom stood ten feet in front of me, her black slacks job-interview crisp, her dark hair as sleek as if she had just come from a salon. We were separated only by a stupid metal gate, but it felt as if she were a million miles away.

"Kid!" The guard sounded less patient now. "You're clear to walk through." I had pulled my curly hair back into a ponytail, but I could feel how wisps in front had fallen out and were now sticking to my forehead. There was sweat running down the small of my back; it was July and hot outside but so cold in the airport the air-conditioned air made my teeth hurt. And my heart was beating louder than a jet engine. I kept gasping for air, but I couldn't seem to get any oxygen. I started to feel dizzy.

"Come on!" There was a teenager behind me, clutching a skateboard. He rolled his eyes. "You're holding up the line!"

I saw my mom gesture to the guard and whisper something to him. I stared at my Keds. I knew what she was saying. *My daughter has an anxiety disorder. Sometimes she has panic attacks and . . .* It was so embarrassing!

The boy behind me gave me a push. I stumbled and almost fell, and by the time I regained my footing, I realized I had taken the few steps through the metal detector and it was over.

I burst into tears. The boy behind me started laughing, and I ran toward the bathroom. I locked myself in a stall and leaned against the cold metal, shaking, not quite sure if I was going to throw up. A minute later, I heard someone else walk in and my mother call, "Becca! Becca!"

"I'm here," I whispered, peeking out through the cracks in the door. My mother was struggling to carry both backpacks and her purse. One strand of her hair was out of place. The bathroom was mercifully deserted.

"You did it," Mom said.

"I made a huge scene!"

"It doesn't matter," she said. "You're through."

"But . . ." I sniveled. "Do I have cancer?"

"Oh, Becca." Mom sighed.

I knew it was ridiculous. But the thought kept bouncing around in my brain. Mom was really good at being patient. She looked in the mirror and combed her fingers through her hair, straightening the one strand. The thought bounced and bounced, like a motorized Ping-Pong ball, until finally, it ran out of steam. I unlocked the door and came out of the stall.

"Here." Mom fumbled in her purse. "Let me give you your Benadryl."

She pulled out a small pill and handed it to me along with a bottle of water. I didn't have a cold or an allergy attack, but, as listed on page 3 of Doomsday Journal #1, Benadryl was sometimes also recommended for anxiety. Especially in kids. It was 1993, for goodness' sake; you'd think they would have invented something better by now! I didn't like taking it—it made my head feel fuzzy and my mouth dry—but I wasn't even on the plane yet, and I was freaking out. I really didn't have a choice.

I felt better as soon as I'd swallowed it. I knew there was no way it could work that fast, but . . . it was part of the plan we'd written out with Dr. Teresa last week. And I wanted to see my father.

So I splashed some water on my face and patted it dry with a scratchy paper towel. We went to McDonald's and each got a Quarter Pounder and fries and a Diet Coke. And as we ate, I tried not to think about the next thing I was afraid of—getting on the plane.

TURN THE PAGE

FOR AN EXCERPT OF

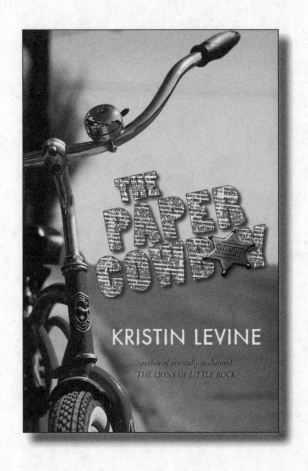

KRISTIN LEVINE

author of critically acclaimed
THE LIONS OF LITTLE ROCK

THE PAPER

"Hands up!"

My best friend, Eddie Sullivan, had a newspaper rolled and pointed at me like a gun. He was only twelve, but over the summer he'd grown so much, he looked big enough to be in high school.

"No way!" I called out. I grabbed the newspaper and tried to wrench it from him. My dog, Boots, started to bark, excited. He was a small, scruffy black mutt, with paws as white as frost on the prairie.

"Surrender, you little commie," Eddie said, "and I might let you live!"

"I'm not a communist!"

Eddie pretended to shoot me with the newspaper.

I fell down, laughing. "Stalin's dead!"

"But the Soviet Union is not giving up. I'm not going to let you take over the world!"

We were standing on a mountain of newspapers. To our right, a glass-bottle hill glowed brown and green in the sunlight. A bit farther on loomed a pile of tin cans, ten feet tall, with the labels burned off so that the metal sparkled like the silver on a sheriff's star.

Eddie grabbed one of my shoes and started to pull. I was laughing so hard, I could barely swat him away. "Help, Boots!"

My dog jumped into the fray, nipping at Eddie's ankles.

It was the day of our community paper drive, when everyone placed their old papers and magazines by the side of the road. Eddie and I had spent all morning following the collection truck, watching his father swing the piles onto the truck bed. After lunch, we followed the truck on our bikes to the scrap yard. The truck would be driven onto a big scale and the homeowners' association would receive a certain amount of money for every pound of paper that had been collected. While we were waiting for our turn on the scale, Eddie and I climbed onto our truck and started poking around.

"You dirty com—" Eddie's voice cracked, so high he sounded like my little sister. He cleared his throat. "You dirty commie," he said, his voice now deep like his father's. Boots sank his teeth into Eddie's shirt and pulled him away. But Eddie didn't let go of my shoe, which came off, and I tumbled down the hill of papers.

We were both laughing so hard, it took me a moment to get my breath. Eddie was standing on top of the pile, holding the shoe over his head like a trophy. Boots was chasing him around in circles, barking. "Victory!" yelled Eddie.

I was about to scramble up the pile and join back in the fight when a headline caught my eye: THE WAR ENDS! Even though it was now September 13, 1953, finding an old newspaper wasn't so unusual. No, it was the masthead that intrigued me: *The Daily Worker*.

"Eddie!" I called. "Come quick!"

Eddie slid down the hill, loose papers flying around him. "What is it, Tommy?"

I held the paper out to him. The *Daily Worker* was a communist newspaper. I knew that from the movies. And I'd found a copy, lying right beside my shoeless foot.

"A commie newspaper!" Eddie's eyes were wide, his cheeks smudged with newsprint.

"Do you know what this means?" I asked.

"What?"

"There's a communist in Downers Grove!" That was the little town where we lived, just a commuter-train ride from Chicago.

Eddie gave me a look.

"Just think about it," I said. "These papers all came from our neighborhood. That means one of our neighbors"—I paused and lowered my voice—"must be a communist."

Eddie looked around, as if he expected to see a Soviet spy parachuting down from the sky. If a Russian caught you, he'd torture you until you agreed to spy on the United States. Sure, it was bad that there was a communist in town, but it was a little bit exciting too. Like when you hear about a fire. You hope no one is hurt and you feel bad if they lost all their belongings. But there's something so thrilling about seeing that fire truck go by with all the bells ringing.

"Is this like the time you convinced everyone the old shack by the pond was haunted and it turned out there were just raccoons inside?" asked Eddie.

3

"No," I protested. "This is proof!" I waved the newspaper.

Eddie's dad yelled at us to get off the truck then. Mr. Sullivan had come back from the war in Korea with a bad limp, but his arms were as thick as the strong man's at the circus. He always helped with the paper drive because no one could swing the stacks of paper onto the truck quite like him.

I rolled up the paper I'd found and stuffed it into my back pocket. Eddie handed me my shoe and I put it on.

"Hey, Tommy," Mr. Sullivan said, "you want to come by and see the bomb shelter I built?"

"Love to," I said. "But I got to get home to dinner."

"It's his birthday," Eddie volunteered. "He's finally twelve like me."

"Well then, happy birthday. Tell your dad we should all go fishing again soon."

"Will do," I said as I jumped on my bike and pedaled off.

You'd think I'd be excited about my birthday. I mean, last week Dad had brought home a box that was just the right shape and size to hold a pair of genuine leather cowboy boots. Mom had promised to make pierogi and I loved the half-circle dumpling noodles filled with mashed potatoes and cheese. There'd probably be an angel food cake too, with a sweet fruit glaze on top.

But Busia, that's Polish for "grandma," wouldn't be there. She'd died a few months before, right about the same time Susie was born. And that's when Mom really started to change. I mean, she'd always been moody, but now she was like a sky full of dark clouds. Sometimes, things would clear right up without a drop of rain, and other times, there'd be lightning and hail. Never quite knowing what the weather would be like at home made my palms sweat.

And as I turned into our driveway and walked my bike to the garage, from inside the house I could already hear screaming.

TURN THE PAGE
FOR AN EXCERPT OF

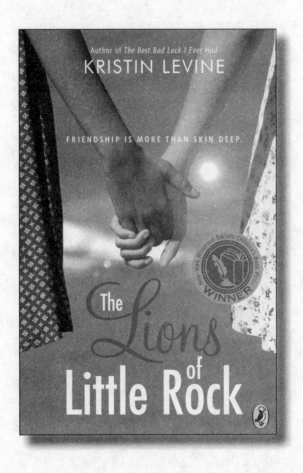

Author of *The Best Bad Luck I Ever Had*

KRISTIN LEVINE

FRIENDSHIP IS MORE THAN SKIN DEEP.

New-York Historical Society Children's Book Prize
WINNER

The *Lions*
of
Little Rock

1

THE HIGH DIVE

I talk a lot. Just not out loud where anyone can hear. At least I used to be that way. I'm no chatterbox now, but if you stop me on the street and ask me directions to the zoo, I'll answer you. Probably. If you're nice, I might even tell you a couple of different ways to get there. I guess I've learned it's not enough to just think things. You have to say them too. Because all the words in the world won't do much good if they're just rattling around in your head.

But I'm getting ahead of myself. To understand me, and how I've changed, I need to go back to 1958.

It was a beautiful day in September and I was standing on top of a diving board. The blue sky was reflected in the water below, the white board felt scratchy under my feet, and the smell of hot dogs wafted up from the snack stand. It was a perfect summer day—the kind you see in the movies—and I was positive I was going to throw up.

You see, it wasn't just any high dive. Oh, no. It was the super-huge, five-meter-high platform diving board, the tallest at Fair Park Swimming Pool, probably the highest in all of Little Rock. It might have even been the highest in all of Arkansas. Which wouldn't have been a problem if I hadn't been afraid of heights. But I was.

Sally McDaniels had told me she was going to jump off and asked if I wanted to come too. Everyone over the age of ten had already jumped off the board a dozen times that summer. Except for me, and I was practically thirteen. It was easier to nod than say no, so there I was.

Sally was waiting behind me on the ladder. Blond and blue-eyed, she wore a pink suit the exact color of her toenails. Sally wasn't really pretty, but no one ever noticed because she acted like she was. "Are you all right?" she asked.

No, of course I wasn't all right. I mean, I wasn't sick or anything, but I was standing perfectly still, frozen as a Popsicle, counting prime numbers in my head. A prime number is a number that can only be divided by itself and one. There are twenty-five of them under a hundred, and reciting them sure does help me when I'm nervous.

"Go ahead and jump," said Sally.

I didn't move. A plane flew across the clouds . . . 2, 3, 5, 7, 11 . . . I wished I were a stork and could fly away. Or a flamingo. Or a penguin. Except I didn't think they flew.

"Marlee," Sally said. "There's a bunch of people behind us."

I hated holding them up, so I took a step toward the edge of the platform . . . 13, 17, 19, 23 . . . but then I got dizzy and fell to my knees.

"Come on," cried the boy on the ladder behind Sally. "Hurry up and jump."

I shook my head and clutched the board . . . 29, 31, 37, 41. It didn't work. I wasn't ever letting go.

Sally laughed. "She said she was really going to do it this time."

I squeezed my eyes tighter and kept counting . . . 43, 47, 53 . . .

2

"Isn't that Judy Nisbett's little sister?" someone said.

It must have only have been a minute or two, but I got all the way to 97 before I felt Judy's hand on my shoulder. "Marlee," she said quietly, "come on down. I already bought a Coke and a PayDay. We can share them on the way home."

I nodded but didn't move.

"Open your eyes," Judy commanded.

I did. Not that I always do what my sister says, but—well, I guess I usually do. In any case, when I saw my sister's clear brown eyes looking at me, I felt much better. She was sixteen and going into the eleventh grade. I could talk to my sister. She was smart and calm and reasonable.

"Do you want me to hold your hand on the way down the ladder?" Judy asked.

I nodded again. It was embarrassing, but I didn't think I could do it on my own. Once I felt her palm on mine, it only took a minute for us to make our way down together.

"What a baby!" said the boy who had been behind me as he brushed past us to climb up again. Sally laughed, and I knew they were right. I was a baby.

"Come on," said Judy. She picked up her book and her bag from the lounge chair where she'd been reading.

"See you at school tomorrow," said her friend Margaret.

"See you," Judy replied, waving good-bye.

Judy hadn't even gotten her hair wet. She'd recently cut it into a short bob and wore it pulled back with a ribbon. My hair was the same brown color as my sister's, but it was long and wavy, and sometimes I still wore it in braids. Sally said I looked like Heidi, but I didn't care. I liked Heidi. She had that nice grandpa and her friend with all those goats.

Goats are okay, but what I really love are wild animals, like

3

the ones you find at the zoo. The Little Rock Zoo was right across the street from the swimming pool. In the gate and down the hill, I knew the lions were pacing in their cages. At night, Judy and I listened to them roar, but during the day they were quiet like me. Judy and I sat on the wall by the zoo entrance as we shared a candy bar and a Coke.

"Sorry," I said. I'd ruined our last day at the pool before school started again.

Judy sighed. "Why are you even friends with Sally McDaniels?"

I shrugged. Sally and I have been friends ever since we were five and she pushed me off the slide at the park.

"She likes to boss you around," Judy said.

That was true. But she was also familiar. I like familiar.

"You need to find a friend you have something in common with," said Judy. "Someone who likes to do the same things you do. That's what . . ."

I stopped listening. I knew all her advice by heart. I needed to find someone who was honest and friendly and nice. I knew all the ways I was supposed to meet this imaginary friend too. *Just say hello. Ask someone a question. Give a compliment.* Maybe it would work, if I could ever figure out the right words.

I know it sounds odd, but I much prefer numbers to words. In math, you always get the same answer, no matter how you do the problem. But with words, *blue* can be a thousand different shades! *Two* is always *two*. I like that.

Judy finally finished lecturing, and I said, "It's easier to put up with Sally. Sometimes she's really nice."

"Yeah," Judy said. "Sometimes."

TURN THE PAGE

FOR AN EXCERPT OF

One brave friendship. One daring plan.

The Best
BAD LUCK
I Ever Had

KRISTIN LEVINE

author of the critically acclaimed THE LIONS OF LITTLE ROCK

1

THE NEW POSTMASTER

I'VE BEEN WRONG BEFORE. OH, HECK, IF I'M being real honest, I've been wrong a lot. But I ain't never been so wrong as I was about Emma Walker. When she first came to town, I thought she was the worst piece of bad luck I'd had since falling in the outhouse on my birthday. I tell you, things were fine in Moundville before Emma got here, least I thought they were. Guess the truth is, you'll never know how wrong I was till I'm done telling and explaining—so I'd better just get on with the story.

My real name is Harry Otis Sims, but everybody calls me Dit. See, when I was little, I used to roll a hoop down Main Street, beating it with a stick as I ran along. One day, two older boys tried to steal my hoop. I hit them with my stick and told them, "Dit away." They laughed. "You talk like a baby. Dit, dit, dit." The name stuck.

There are ten children in our family: Della, Ollie, Ulman, Elman, Raymond, me, Earl, Pearl, Robert and Lois. That's just too many kids. There are never leftovers at supper, and you never get new clothes. We don't even get to go to the store for shoes: Mama just keeps them all in a big old barrel. When

1

the pair you're wearing gets too tight, you throw yours in and pick out another one. With so many kids, sometimes I think my pa don't even know my name, since it's always, "Della, Ollie, Ulman, Elman, Raymond, uh, I mean Dit."

We all live in a big old house that Pa built himself right off Main Street in Moundville, Alabama. Most of the people in Moundville are farmers like my pa. Just about everything grows well in our rich, dark soil, but especially corn and cotton. Before I even had my nickname, Pa taught me how to count by showing me the number of ears of corn to feed the mule.

Most evenings my whole family, and just about everybody in town, gathers in front of Mrs. Pooley's General Goods Store to wait for the train. Mrs. Pooley is the meanest old lady I've ever met. She smokes, spits and has a temper shorter than a bulldog's tail. But her store has a wide, comfortable porch and a great view of the train depot, just across the street. The evening Emma came, Mrs. Pooley sat in her usual rocker, smoking a pipe with Uncle Wiggens.

Uncle Wiggens ain't really my uncle, everyone just calls him that. He's over eighty and fought in the War Between the States. He only has one leg and one hero, General Robert E. Lee. Uncle Wiggens manages to work Lee's name into pretty much any old conversation. You might say, "My, it's cold today," and he'd reply, "You think this is cold? General Lee said it didn't even qualify as chill till your breath froze on your nose and made a little icicle." He had about five different stories of how he lost his leg, every one of them entertaining.

That night I was listening to the version that involved him running five Yankees into a bear's den as I wound a ball of twine into a baseball. Course if I'd had the money, I could have

2

bought a new ball at Mrs. Pooley's store, but if you wind twine real careful, it's almost as good as a real ball.

The new postmaster was coming to town, and the grown-ups were as wound up as the kids on Christmas. The postmaster was in charge of sorting and delivering the mail, but he also sent and received telegrams. This meant he knew any good gossip long before anybody else. The last postmaster had been a lazy good-for-nothing: everyone had gotten the wrong mail two days late. He and his family had finally skipped town for refusing to pay their debts at Mrs. Pooley's store.

I was excited too. The new postmaster, Mr. Walker, was supposed to have a boy who was twelve, just like me. I sure hoped he liked to play baseball. It was June 1917, and my best friend, Chip, had just left to spend the summer with his grandma in Selma.

My ball of twine got bigger and bigger till there was a small light, far off in the distance. We all jumped up and ran across the street to the train depot. There was a flash of copper as the golden eagle on the top of the huge locomotive flew out of the night sky. The whistle howled, white steam poured out of the engine and the train came to a slow stop in front of the station.

A few local men who worked in Tuscaloosa got off first. Next, a couple of townspeople who had been visiting relatives climbed down the steps. Finally, a thin girl nobody knew appeared in the doorway of the train.

The girl looked about my age and wore a fancy navy dress. Her hair was carefully combed and pulled back into a neat braid, tied with a red ribbon. She clutched a small suitcase of smooth leather. She was also colored.

ACKNOWLEDGMENTS

THERE ARE SO many people I need to thank for this book. First of all, I want to thank my editor, Stacey Barney, and my agent, Kathy Green, for their extreme patience as I worked my way through more drafts and revisions than I ever expected. This was our fourth book together—it's a lovely thing to have colleagues you can trust and count on (and actually like as people—let's hang out again soon!).

My writing group, Pamela Ehrenberg, Caroline Hickey, Tammar Stein, and Elizabeth Brokamp, offered support and encouragement, and helped me believe I would eventually find and finish this story.

And where would I be without all the people who helped me with research and notes as advance readers?! Jim McAlister, Deborah DiMarzio, William Dye, Monika Waclawski, Paula Ketchel, Cherrise Boucher, Suzy Carpenter, Kim Johnson, Tyler Johnson, Taylor Johnson, Kristin Carlsen Meek, Anna K. Meek, Riley Neubauer, Kenneth R. Hewitt, Jimmy Powers, Adam Levine (my ex-husband—sorry, music fans, not the singer), and Kimberly Brooks Mazella (and all the wonderful ladies I met through her group) generously shared their thoughts and comments. Among my dear friends who read early drafts are Debbie Gaydos, Jessie Auten, Marcos Bolaños (who first got me thinking about using jigsaw puzzles in the story), and Juan Carlos Perez-Tolentino, as well as the many others who routinely asked me, "How's the book coming?" without fail for years.

The team at Putnam is always amazing. A special shout-out to Kate Meltzer, Kaitlin Kneafsey, Courtney Gilfillian, Cindy Howle and Ana Deboo for copyediting, Tony Sahara for the cover, and Eileen Savage for the design.

Thank you also to all the schools and libraries that have invited me to come speak over the past few years, as well as all the people who have taken the time to write and let me know that they have enjoyed my books. Writing can be a lonely profession—your belief, support, and enthusiasm have kept me going.

My parents, Marlene and Tom Walker, have supported my work since I took my first writing class. And when the kids get sick right before a deadline, well, who else can you call except the grandparents?! Thank you for nursing us all through any number of colds, flus, and bouts of strep throat. A big thank-you to my sister, Erika Knott, who recently discovered the joy of reading through audiobooks, for reading my manuscript and giving her thoughts and support as well.

Most of all, I want to thank my amazing daughters, Charlotte and Kara. There have been a lot of changes in our family in the past five years and you've weathered them all with grace, compassion, and resilience. Thank you for watching that extra hour of TV when I needed to get "just one more thing done," texting me funny emojis when I'm on a business trip, and even giving me your own comments and thoughts on this manuscript. Whether we're having family reading time while eating our bedtime snack or snuggling on the couch watching *Doctor Who*, I feel so lucky to have the honor and privilege of being your mother.

Jennifer Brooks

KRISTIN LEVINE lives in Alexandria, Virginia, with her daughters, two bunnies, and one cat. A lifelong learner, Kristin studied German at Swarthmore College, Film and Video at American University, and is currently pursuing a degree in Data Science at George Washington University. She loves visiting schools and talking with young people about the writing process. Her most recent novel, *The Thing I'm Most Afraid Of,* was inspired by a gap year she spent in Vienna, Austria, working as an au pair.

You can visit Kristin Levine at kristinlevine.com